OFFICIALLY NOTED

Stained pocket page 7/14

LIBRARIAN REVIEWER
Laurie K. Holland
Media Specialist (National Board Certified), Edina, MN
MA in Elementary Education, Minnesota State University, Mankato, MN

READING CONSULTANT
Elizabeth Stedem
Educator/Consultant, Colorado Springs, CO
MA in Elementary Education, University of Denver, CO

Graphic Sparks are published by Stone Arch Books,
151 Good Counsel Drive, P.O. Box 669,
Mankato, Minnesota 56002.
www.stonearchbooks.com

Copyright © 2006 by Stone Arch Books.

Library of Congress Cataloging-in-Publication Data
Nickel, Scott.
    Blast to the Past / by Scott Nickel; illustrated by Steve Harpster.
    p. cm. — (Graphic Sparks)
    ISBN-13: 978-1-59889-033-4 (hardcover)
    ISBN-10: 1-59889-033-6 (hardcover)
    1. Graphic novels. I. Harpster, Steve. II. Title. III. Series.
PN6727.N544B63 2006
741.5—dc22   2005026646

Summary: David's geeky brother Darrin invents a time machine in his bedroom. Now David
and his buddy Ben can zip back a few days to retake that test they flunked. But time travel is
tricky. Instead of zapping back to history class, the boys might just become history!

Art Director: Heather Kindseth
Production Manager: Sharon Reid
Production/Design: James Liebman, Mie Tsuchida
Production Assistance: Bob Horvath, Eric Murray

1 2 3 4 5 6 11 10 09 08 07 06

Printed in the United States of America.

BY SCOTT NICKEL

ILLUSTRATED BY STEVE HARPSTER

STONE ARCH BOOKS
MINNEAPOLIS   SAN DIEGO

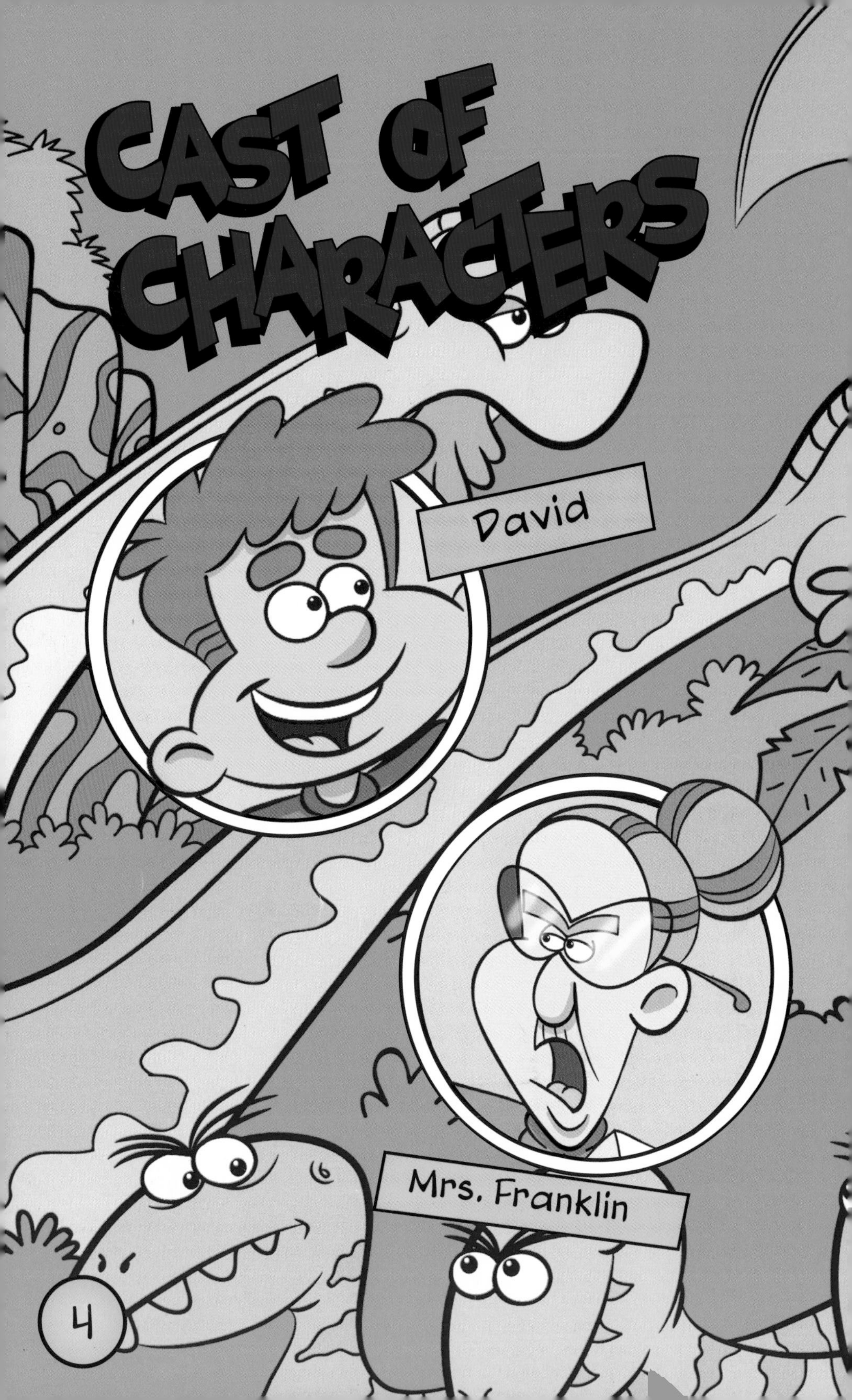
CAST OF CHARACTERS
David
Mrs. Franklin

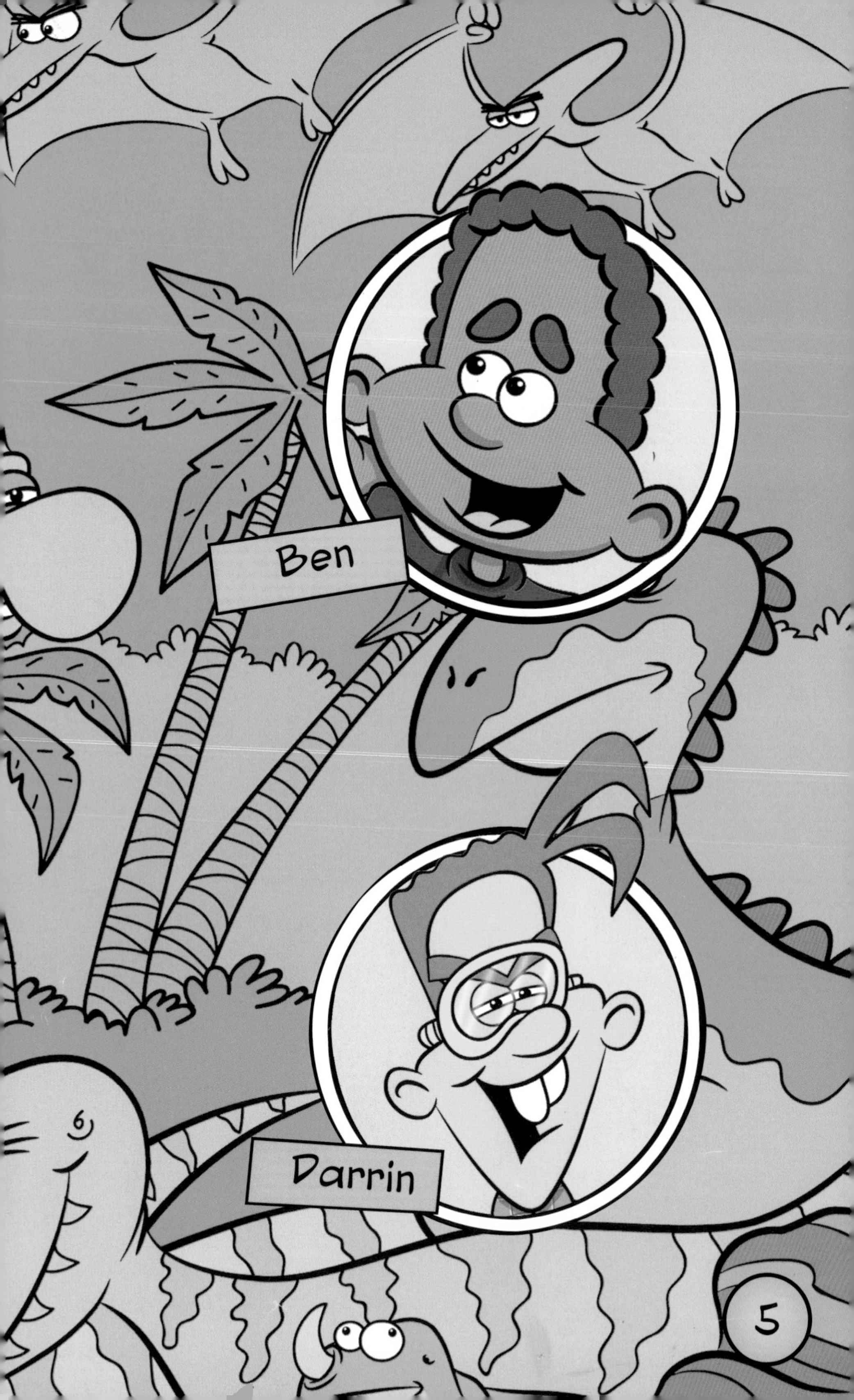
Ben
Darrin

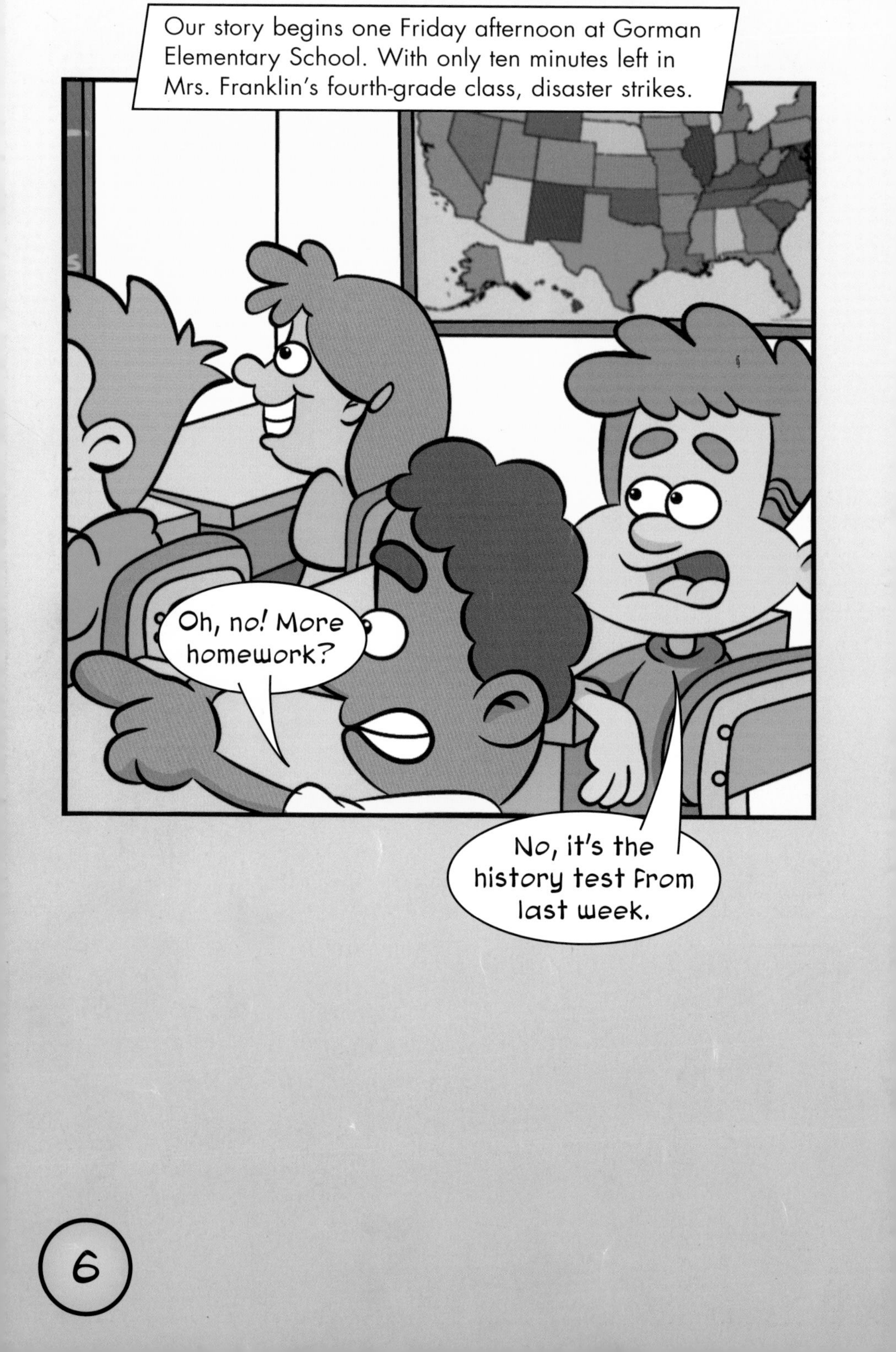
Our story begins one Friday afternoon at Gorman Elementary School. With only ten minutes left in Mrs. Franklin's fourth-grade class, disaster strikes.
Oh, no! More homework?
No, it's the history test from last week.

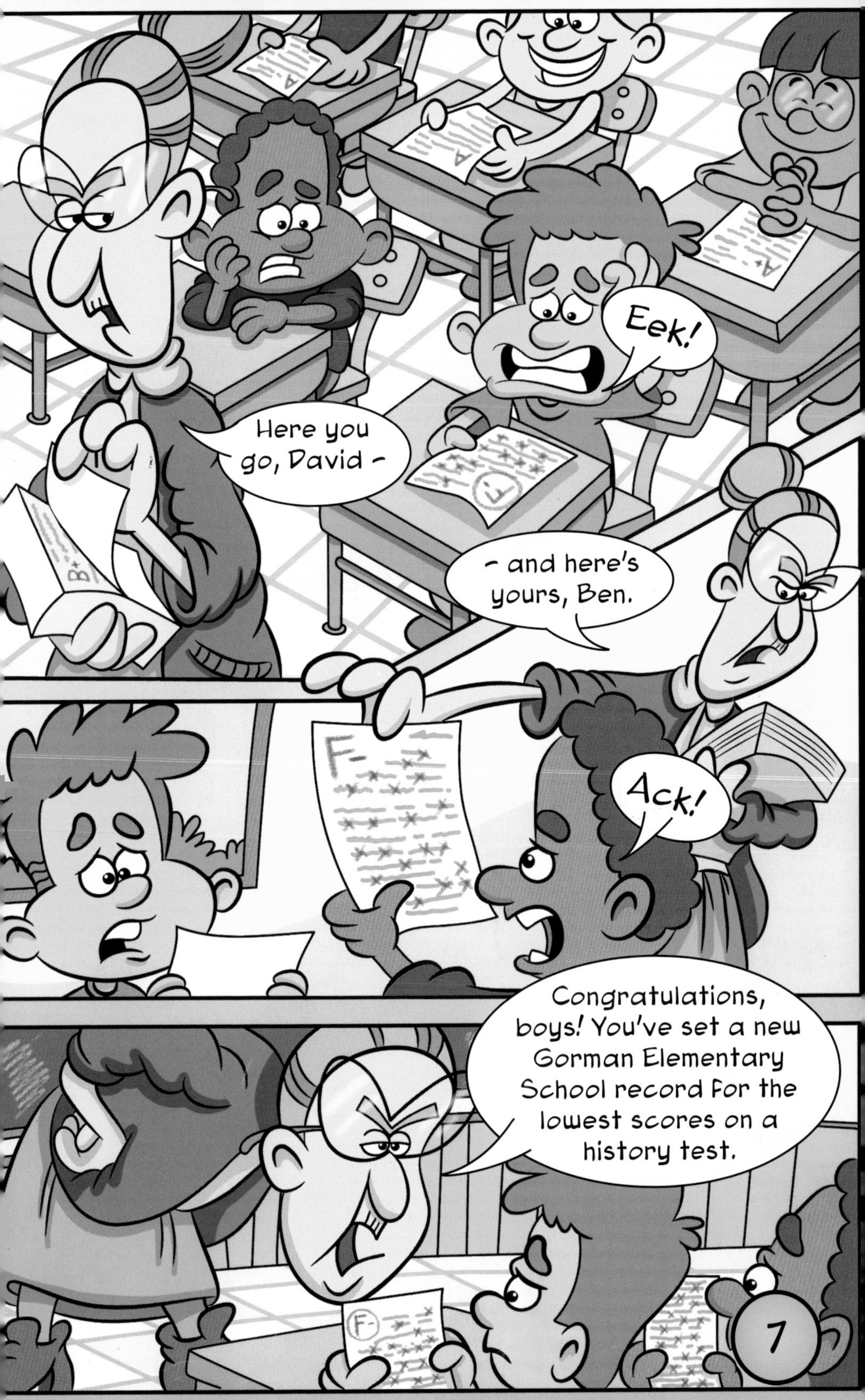
Eek!
Here you go, David -
- and here's yours, Ben.
Ack!
Congratulations, boys! You've set a new Gorman Elementary School record for the lowest scores on a history test.

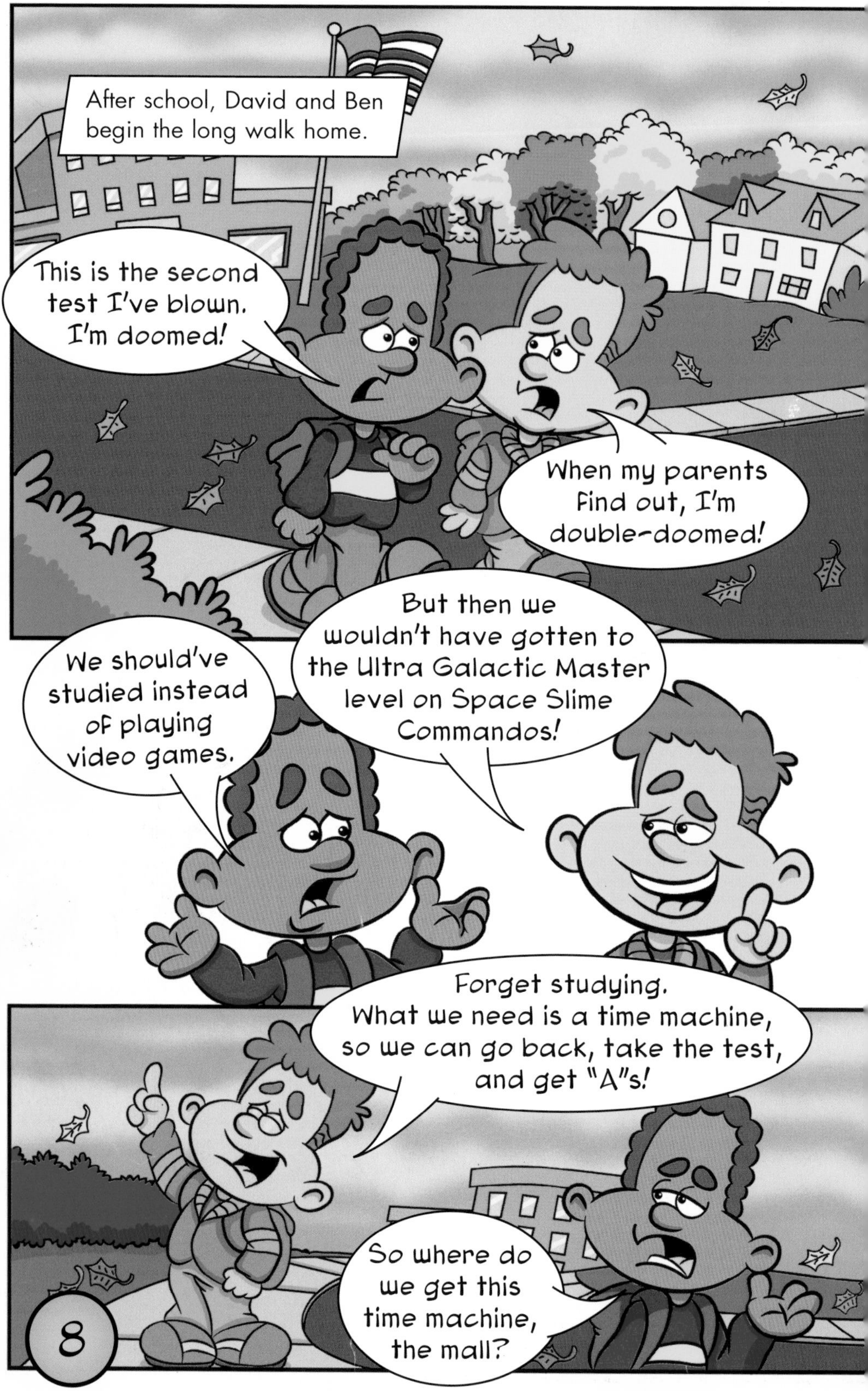
After school, David and Ben begin the long walk home.
This is the second test I've blown. I'm doomed!
When my parents find out, I'm double-doomed!
We should've studied instead of playing video games.
But then we wouldn't have gotten to the Ultra Galactic Master level on Space Slime Commandos!
Forget studying. What we need is a time machine, so we can go back, take the test, and get "A"s!
So where do we get this time machine, the mall?

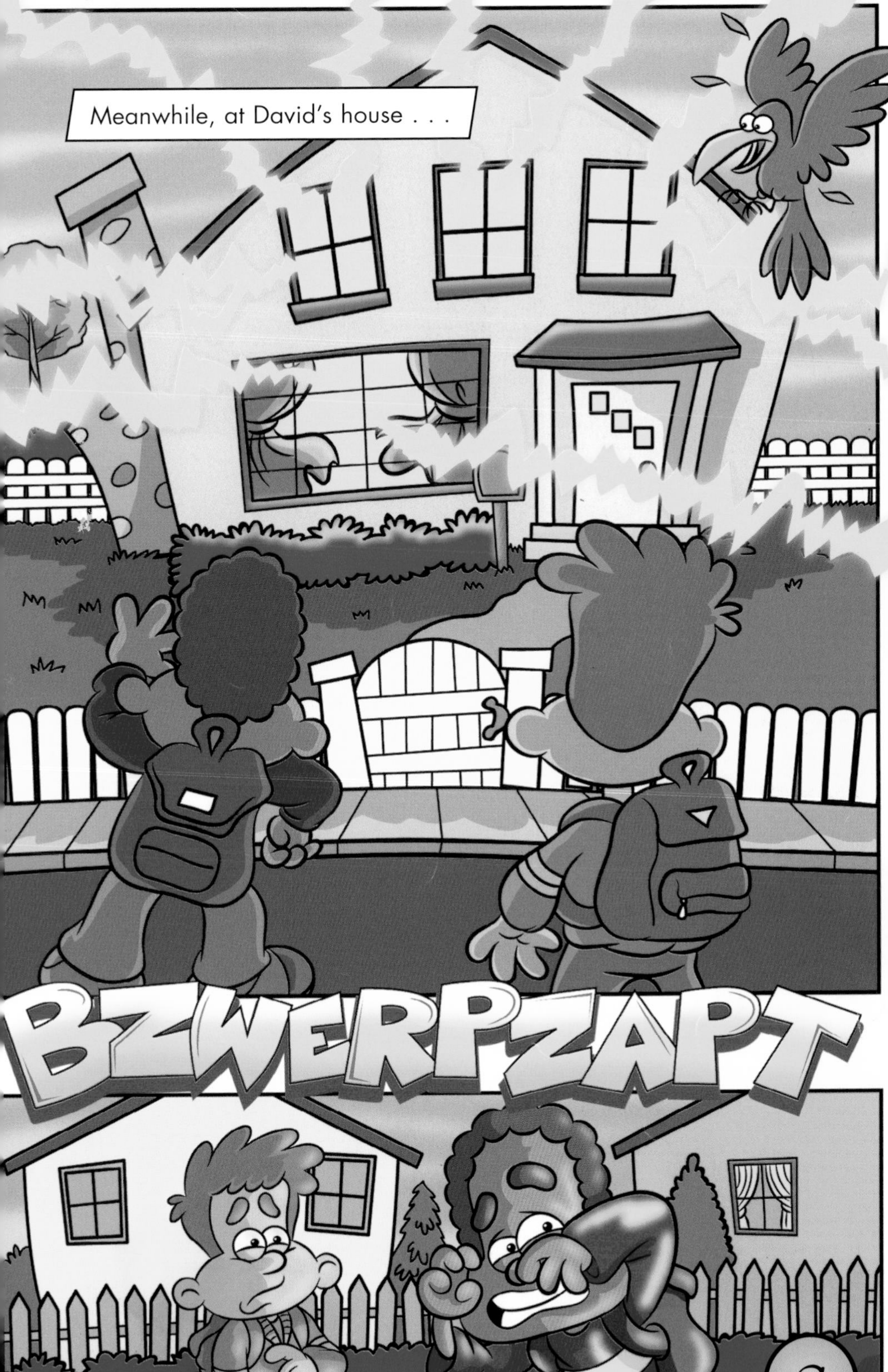
Meanwhile, at David's house . . .
BZWERPZAPT

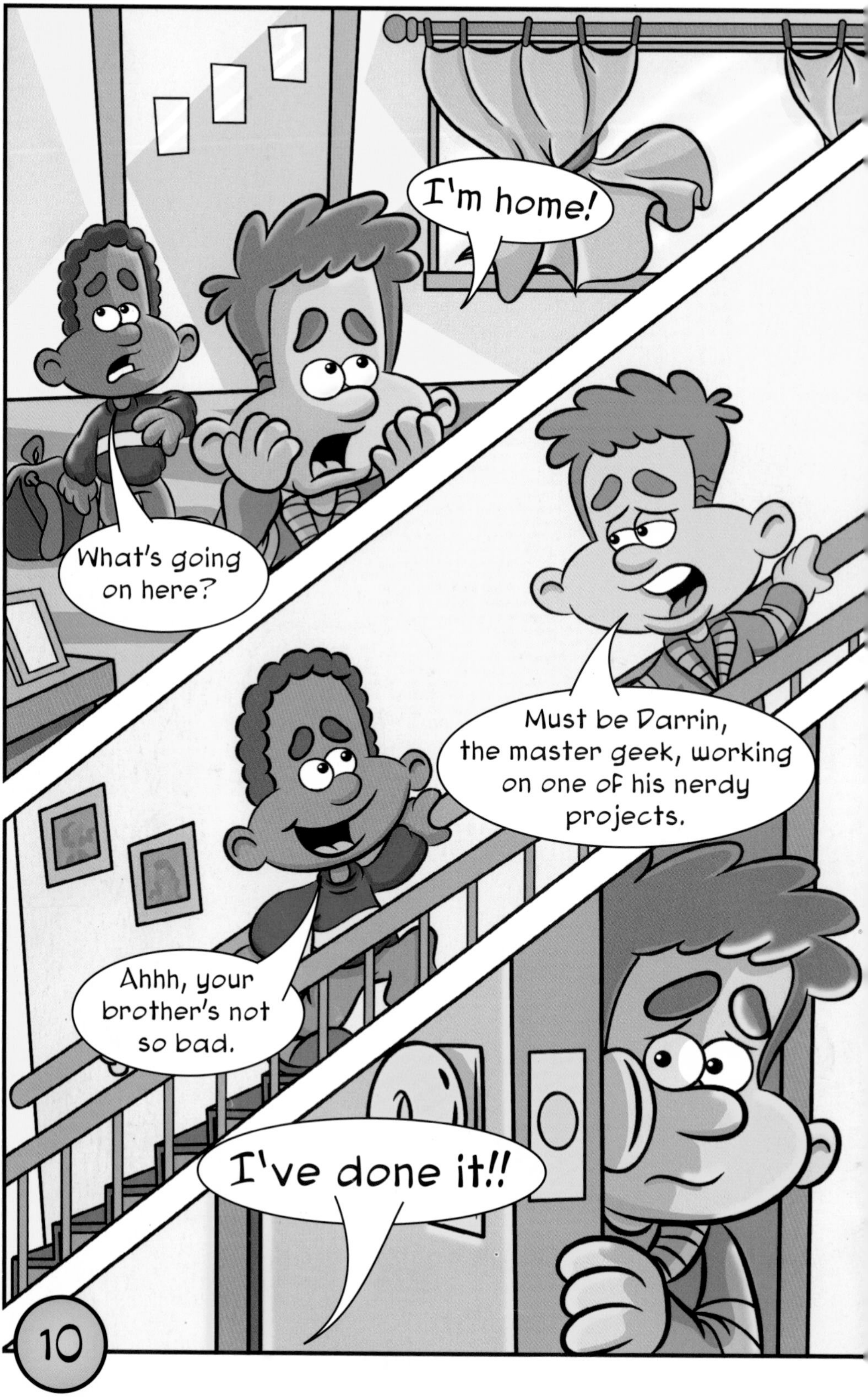
I'm home!
What's going on here?
Must be Darrin, the master geek, working on one of his nerdy projects.
Ahhh, your brother's not so bad.
I've done it!!

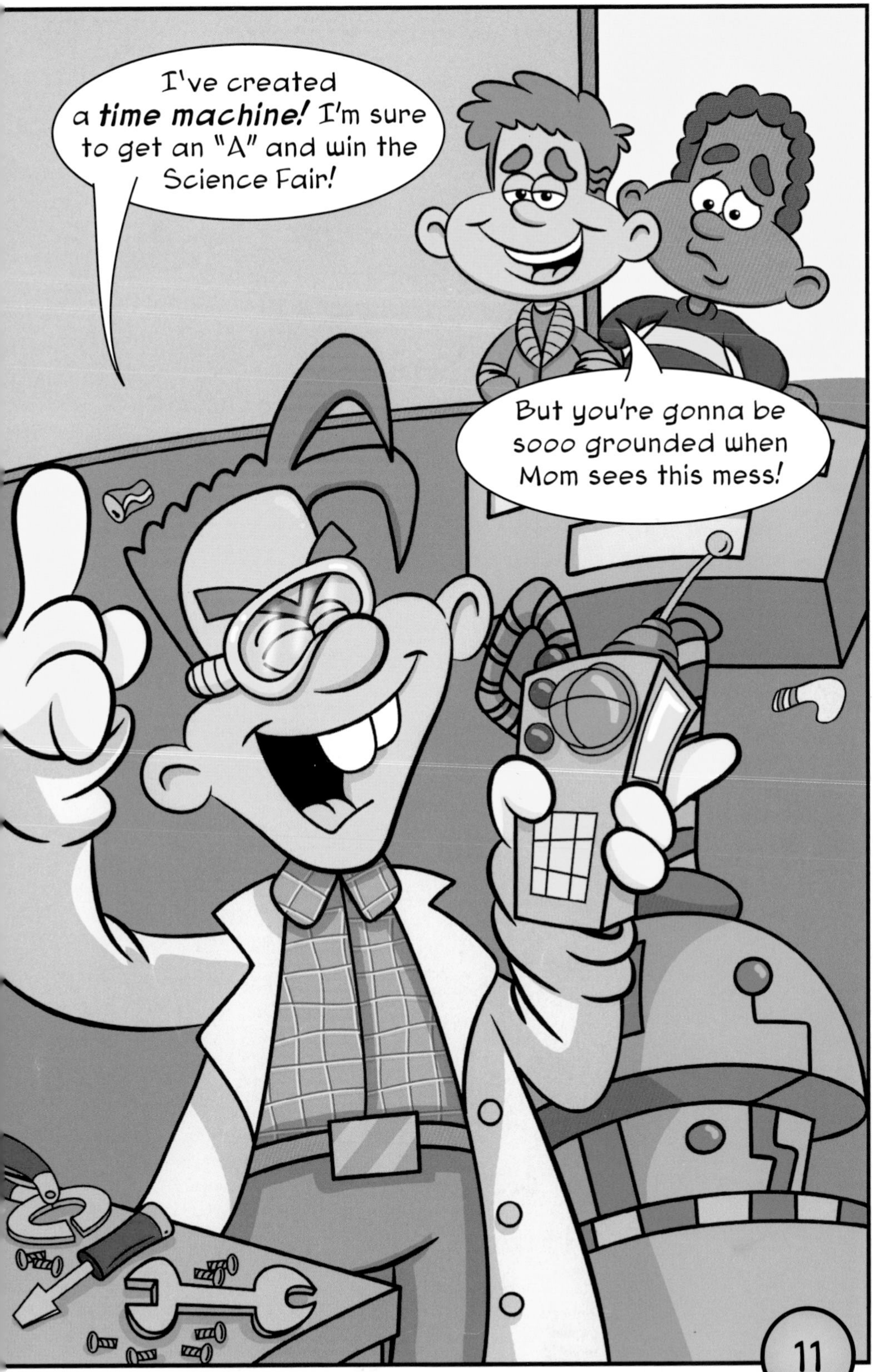
I've created a ***time machine!*** I'm sure to get an "A" and win the Science Fair!
But you're gonna be sooo grounded when Mom sees this mess!

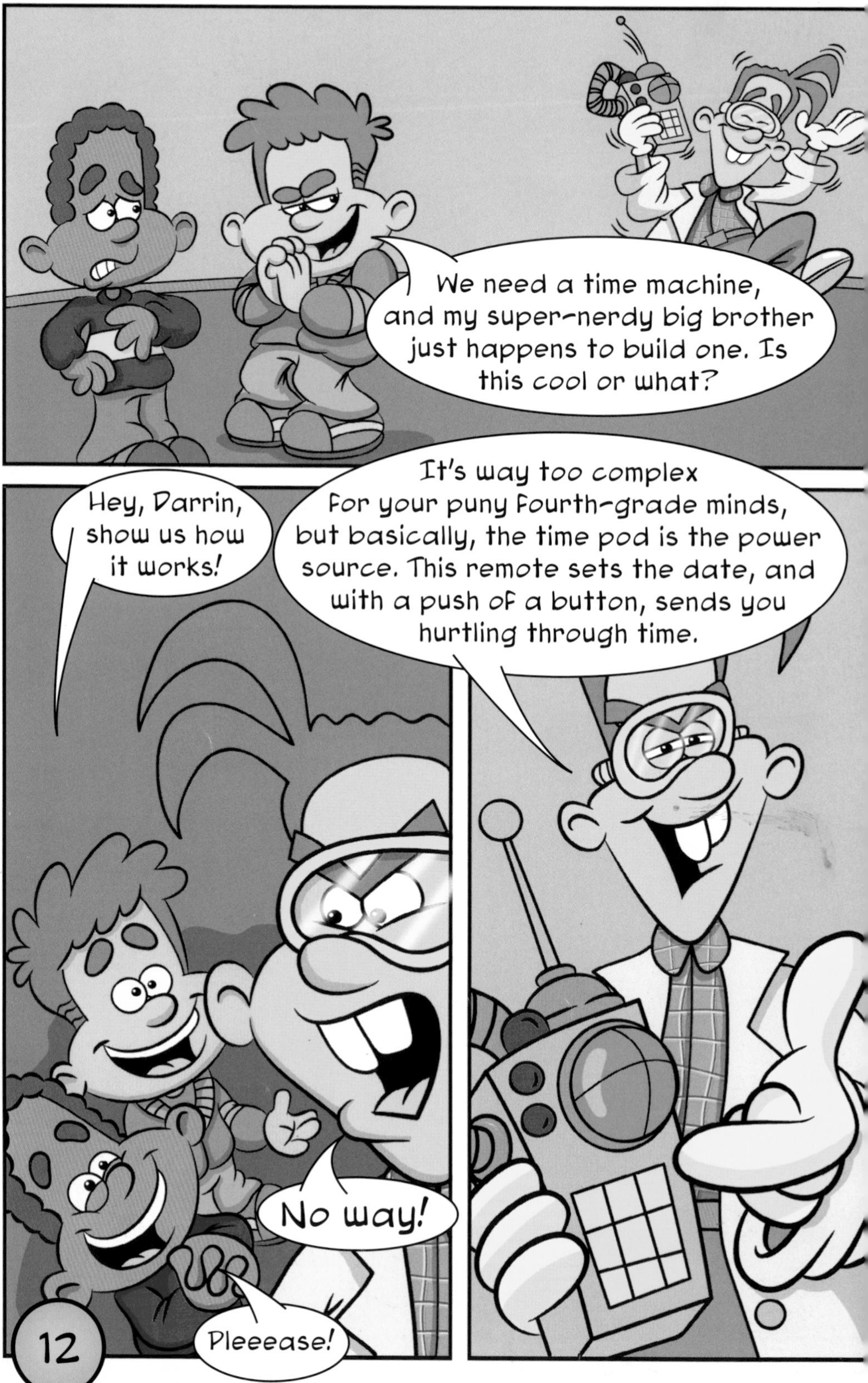
We need a time machine, and my super-nerdy big brother just happens to build one. Is this cool or what?
Hey, Darrin, show us how it works!
No way!
Pleeease!
It's way too complex for your puny fourth-grade minds, but basically, the time pod is the power source. This remote sets the date, and with a push of a button, sends you hurtling through time.

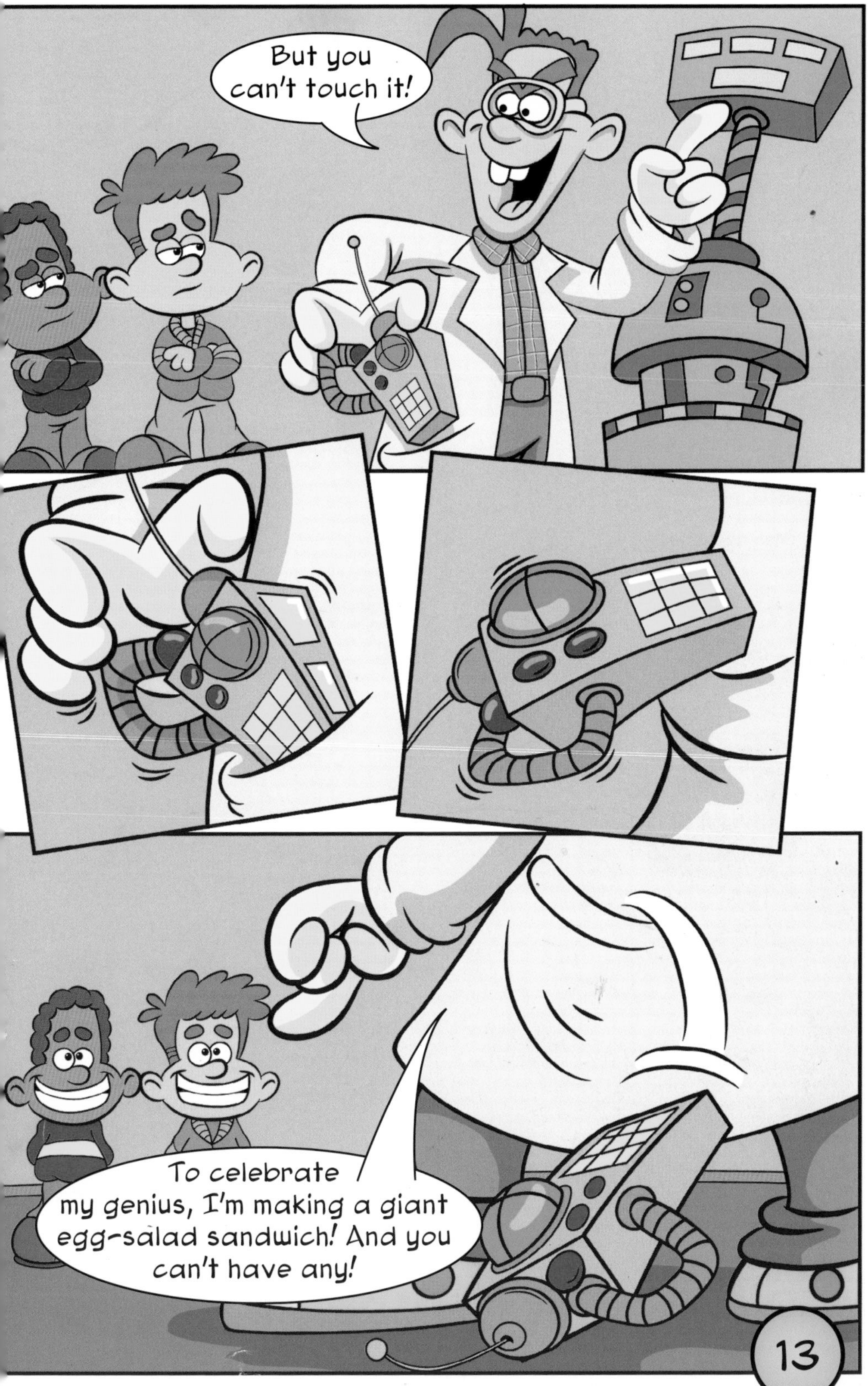

But you can't touch it!
To celebrate my genius, I'm making a giant egg-salad sandwich! And you can't have any!

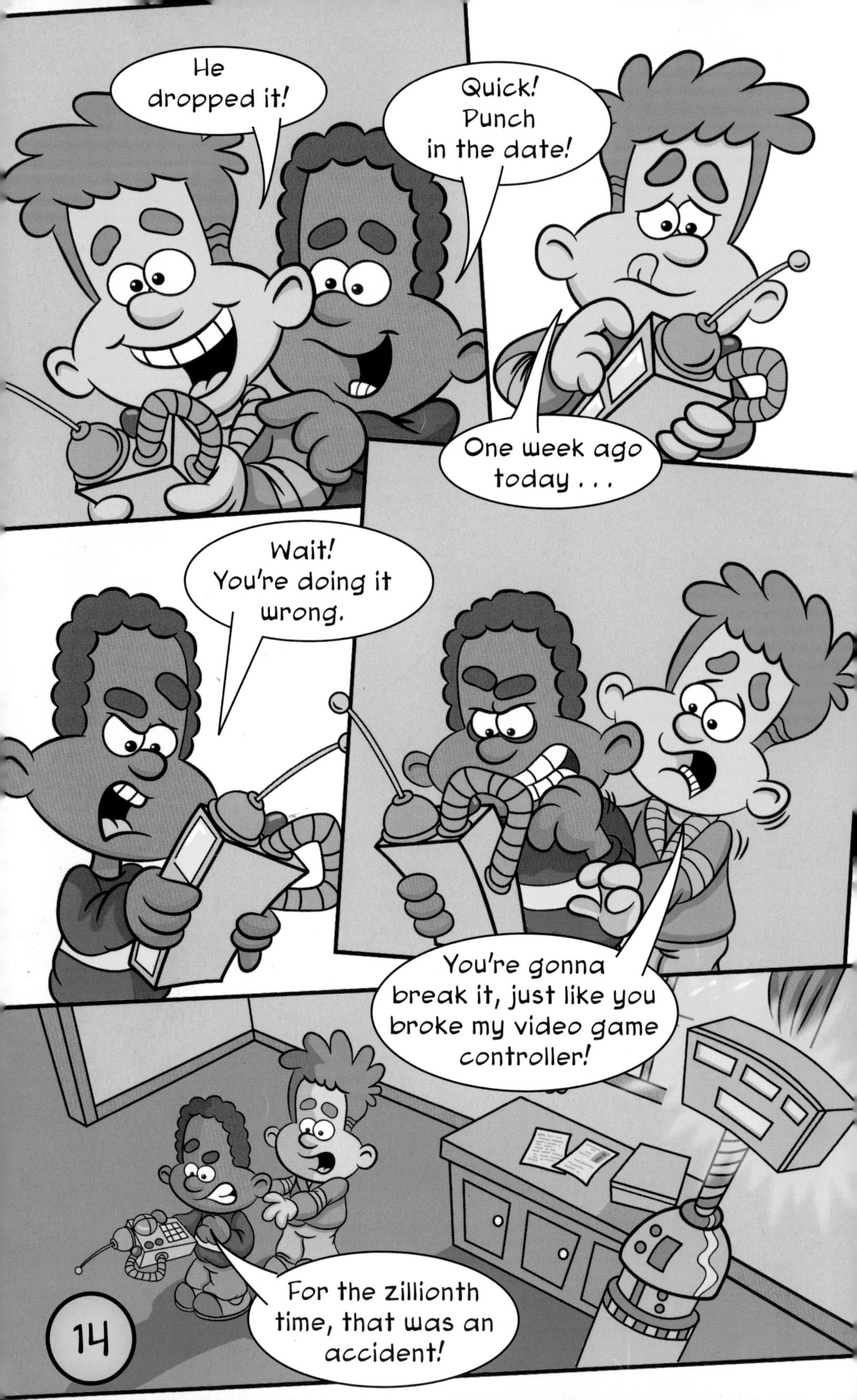
He dropped it!
Quick! Punch in the date!
One week ago today . . .
Wait! You're doing it wrong.
You're gonna break it, just like you broke my video game controller!
For the zillionth time, that was an accident!

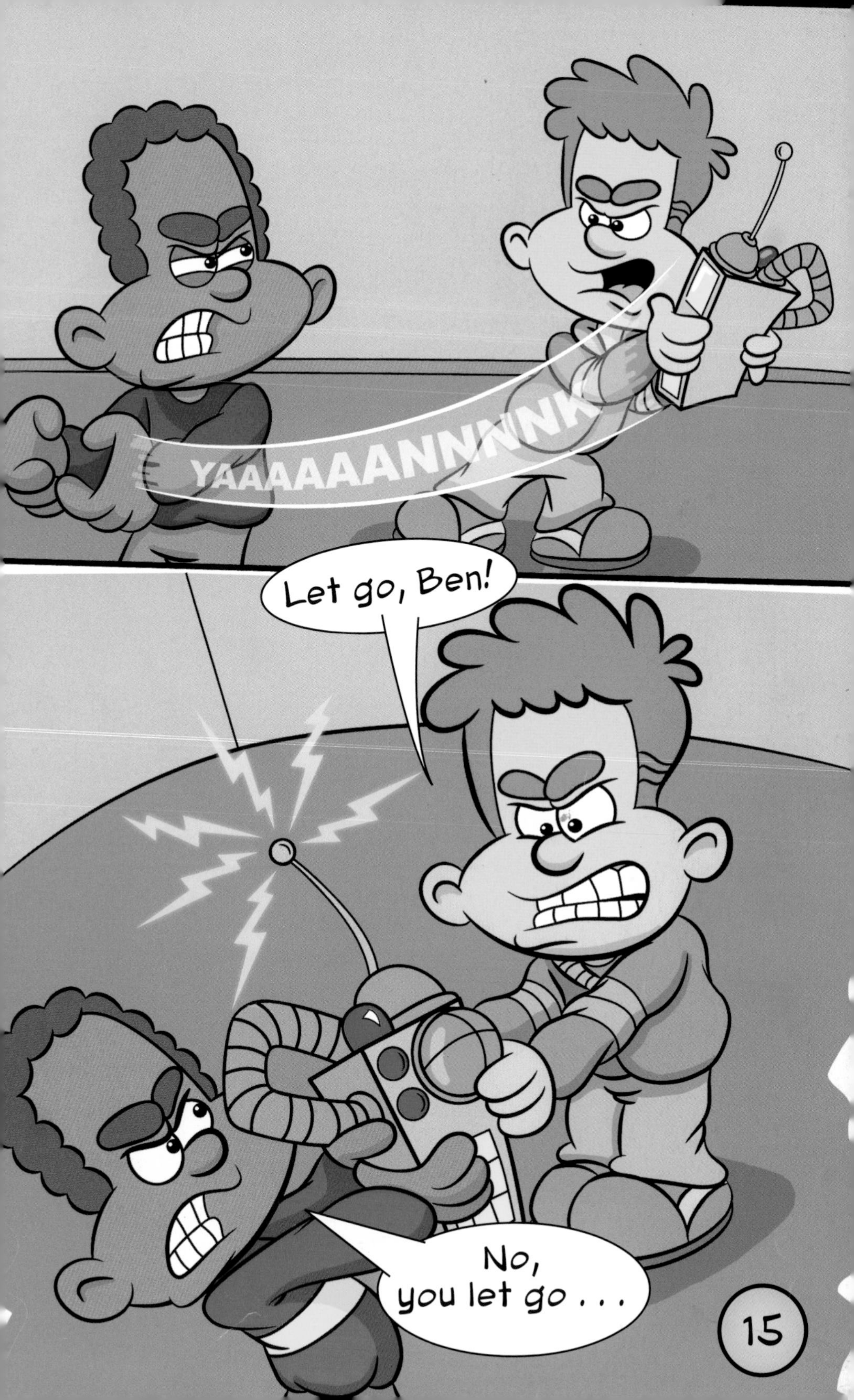
YAAAAAANNNNNK
Let go, Ben!
No,
you let go . . .

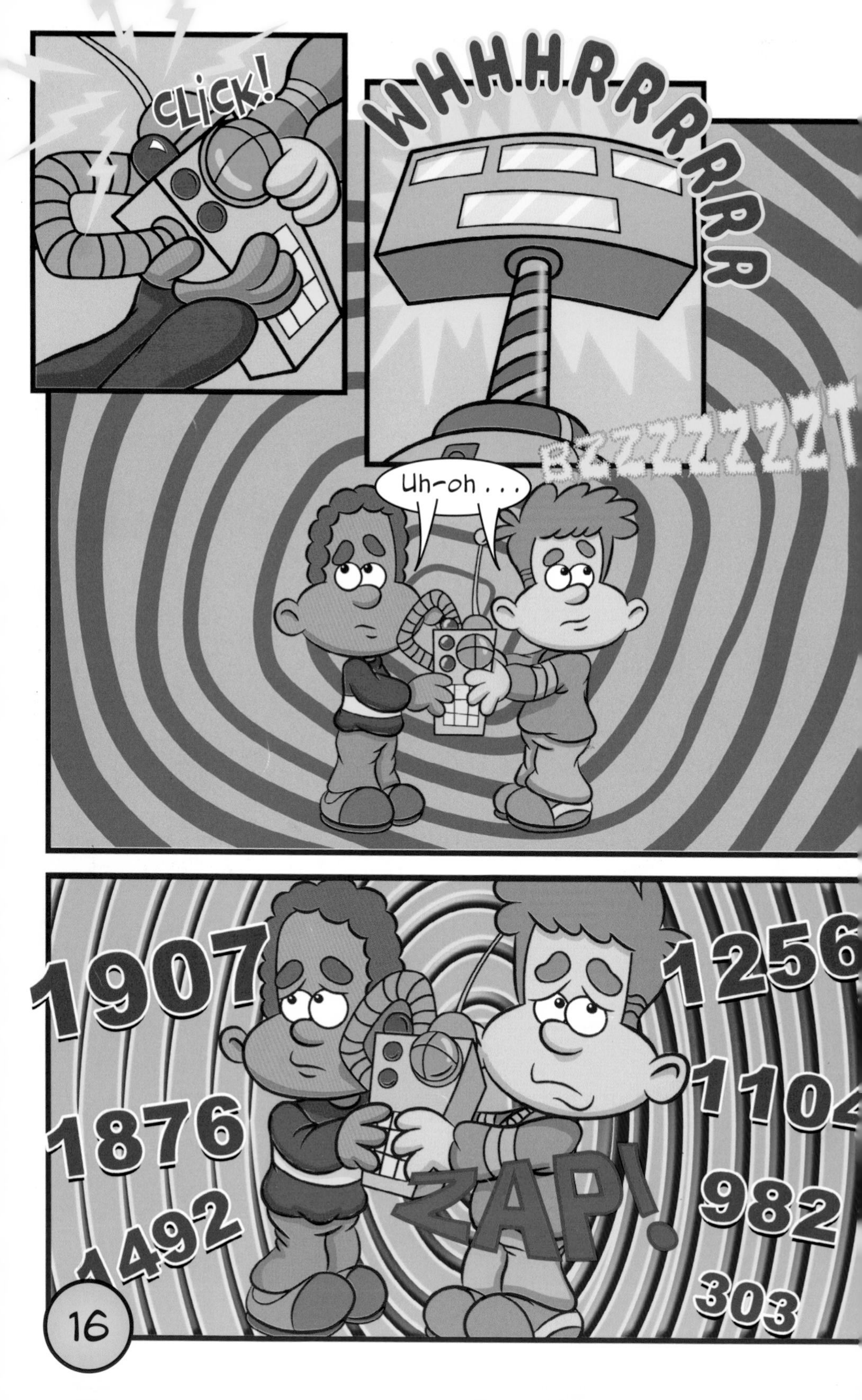
CLICK!
WHHHRRRRRRR
BZZZZZZZZT
Uh-oh . . .
1907
1256
1876
1104
1492
ZAP!
982
303

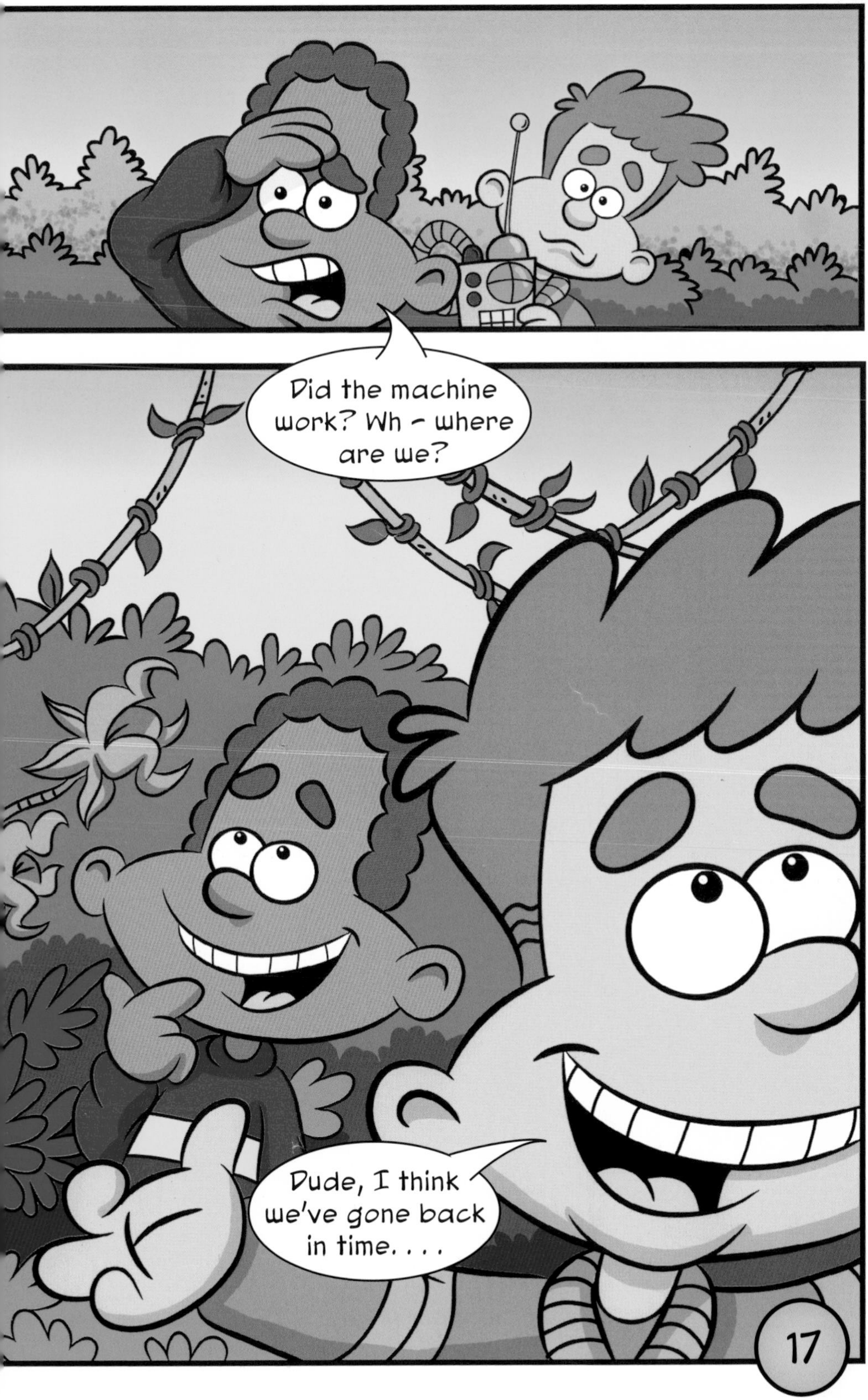
Did the machine work? Wh - where are we?
Dude, I think we've gone back in time. . . .

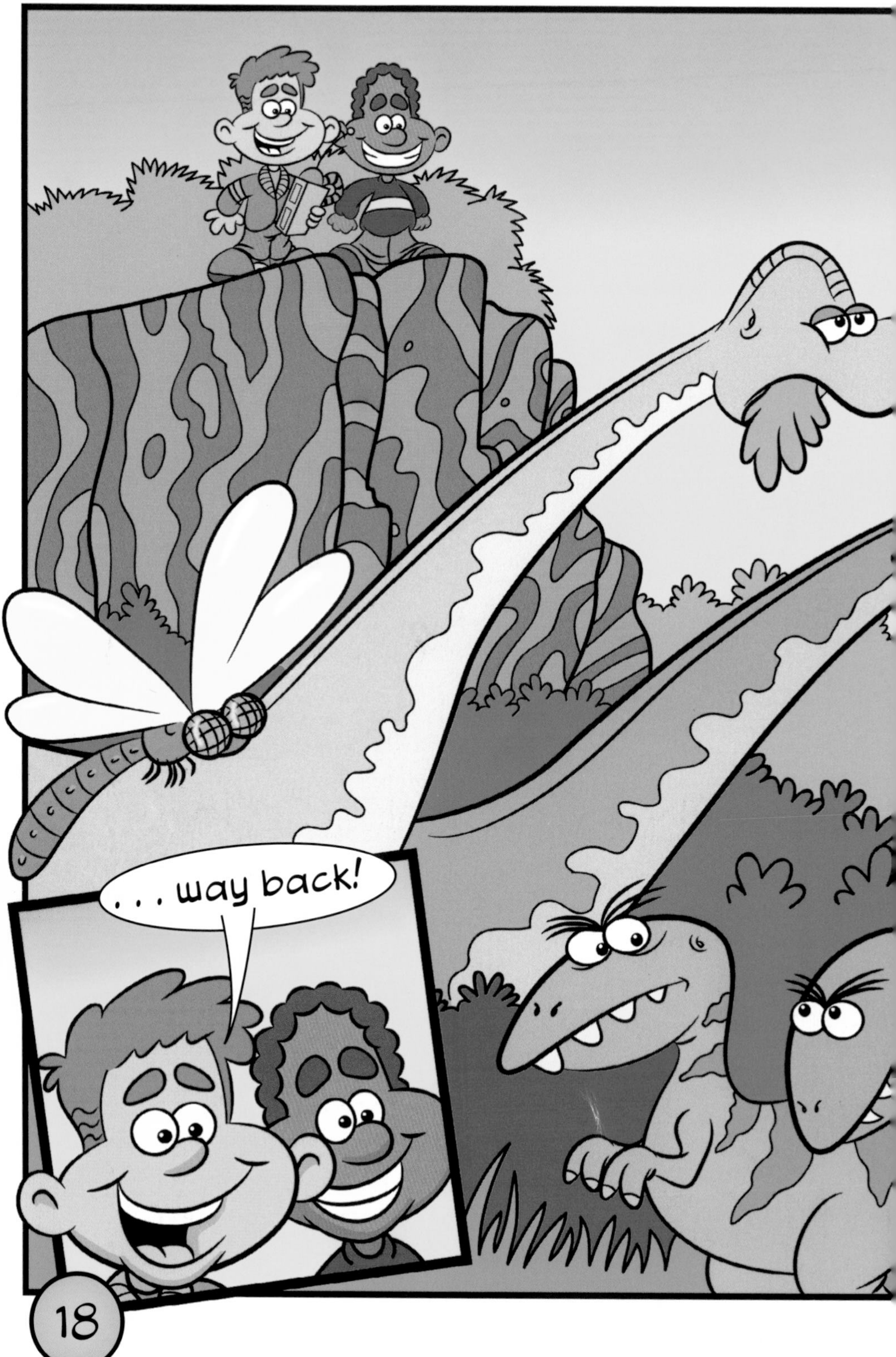
. . . way back!

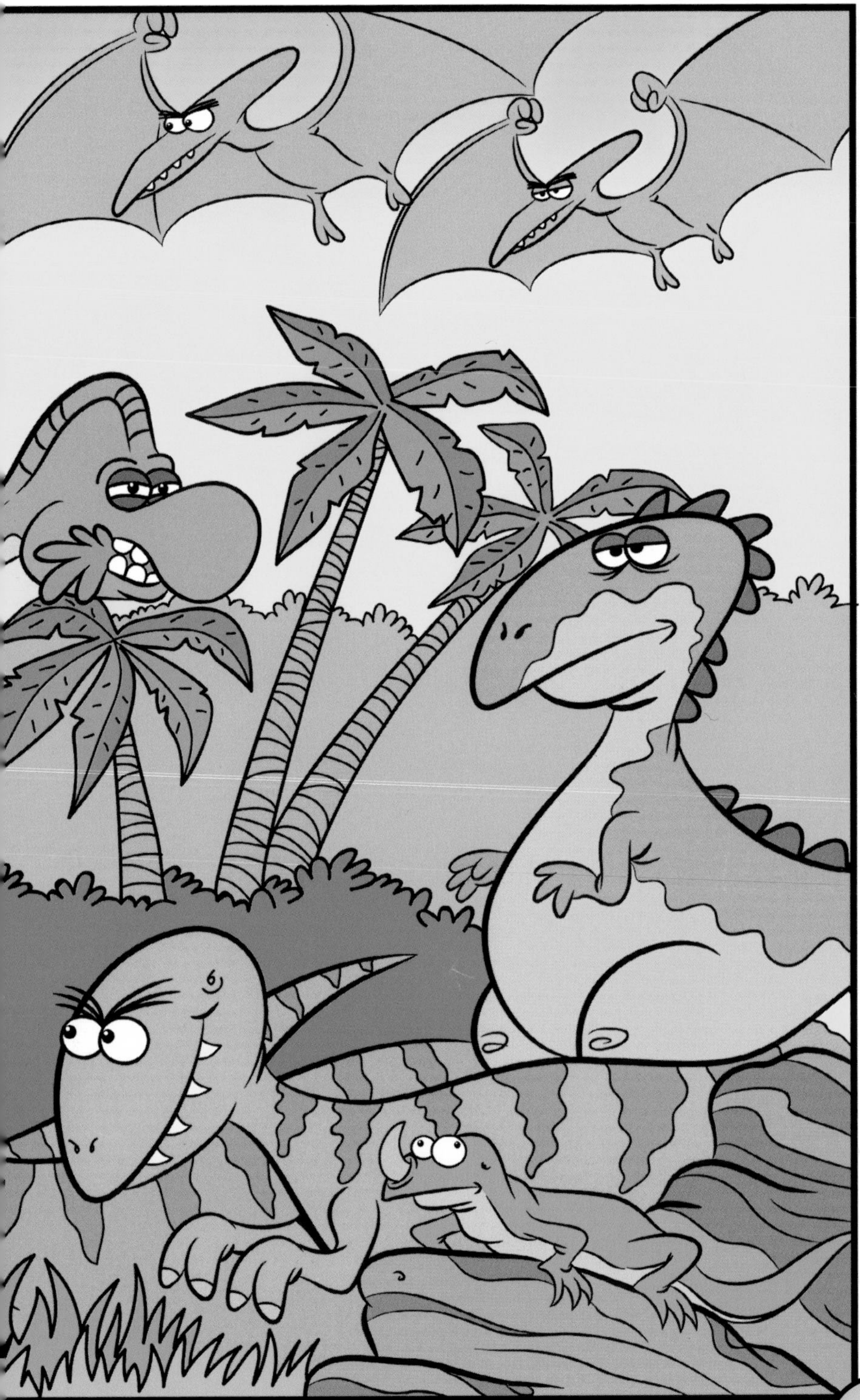

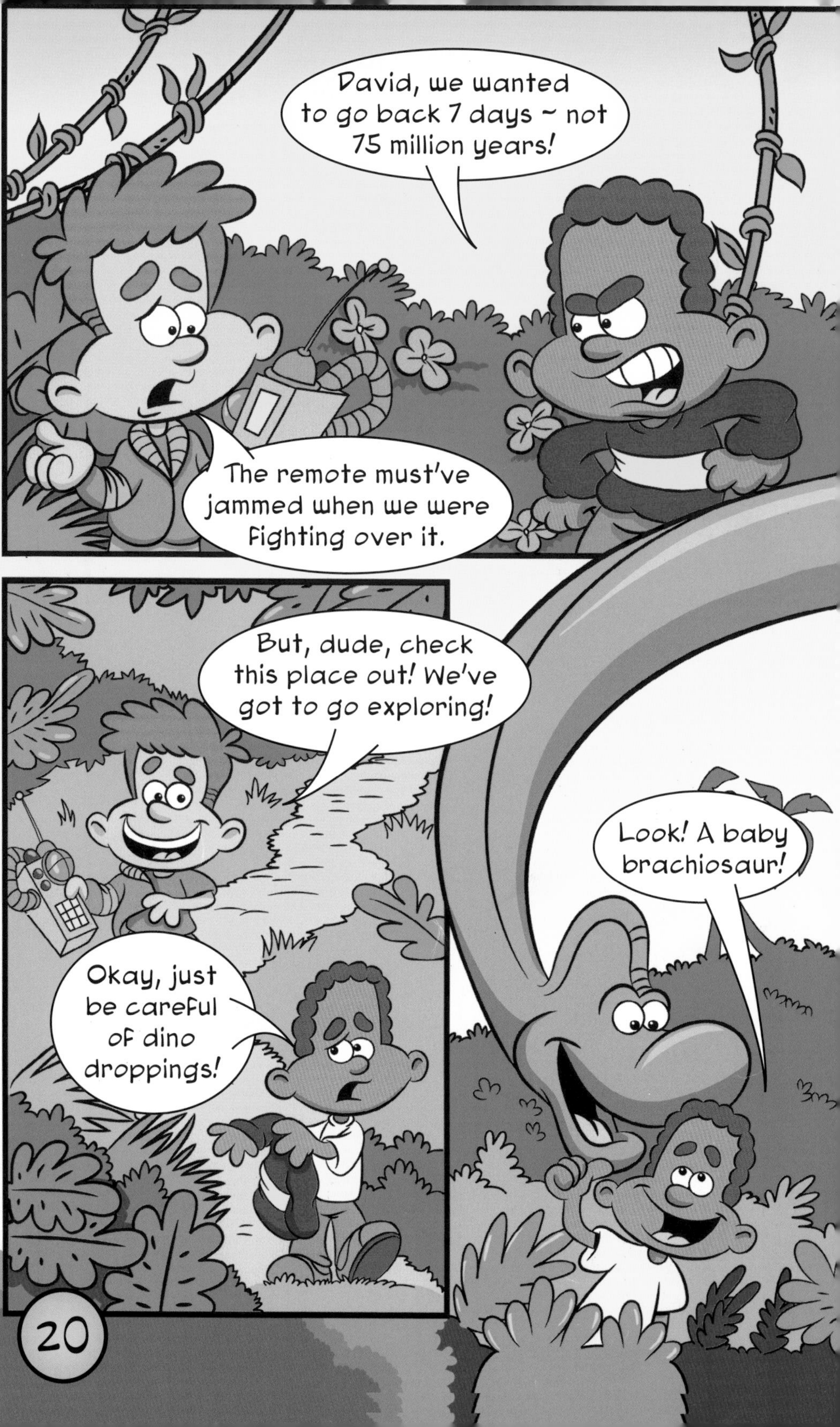
David, we wanted to go back 7 days ~ not 75 million years!
The remote must've jammed when we were fighting over it.
But, dude, check this place out! We've got to go exploring!
Okay, just be careful of dino droppings!
Look! A baby brachiosaur!

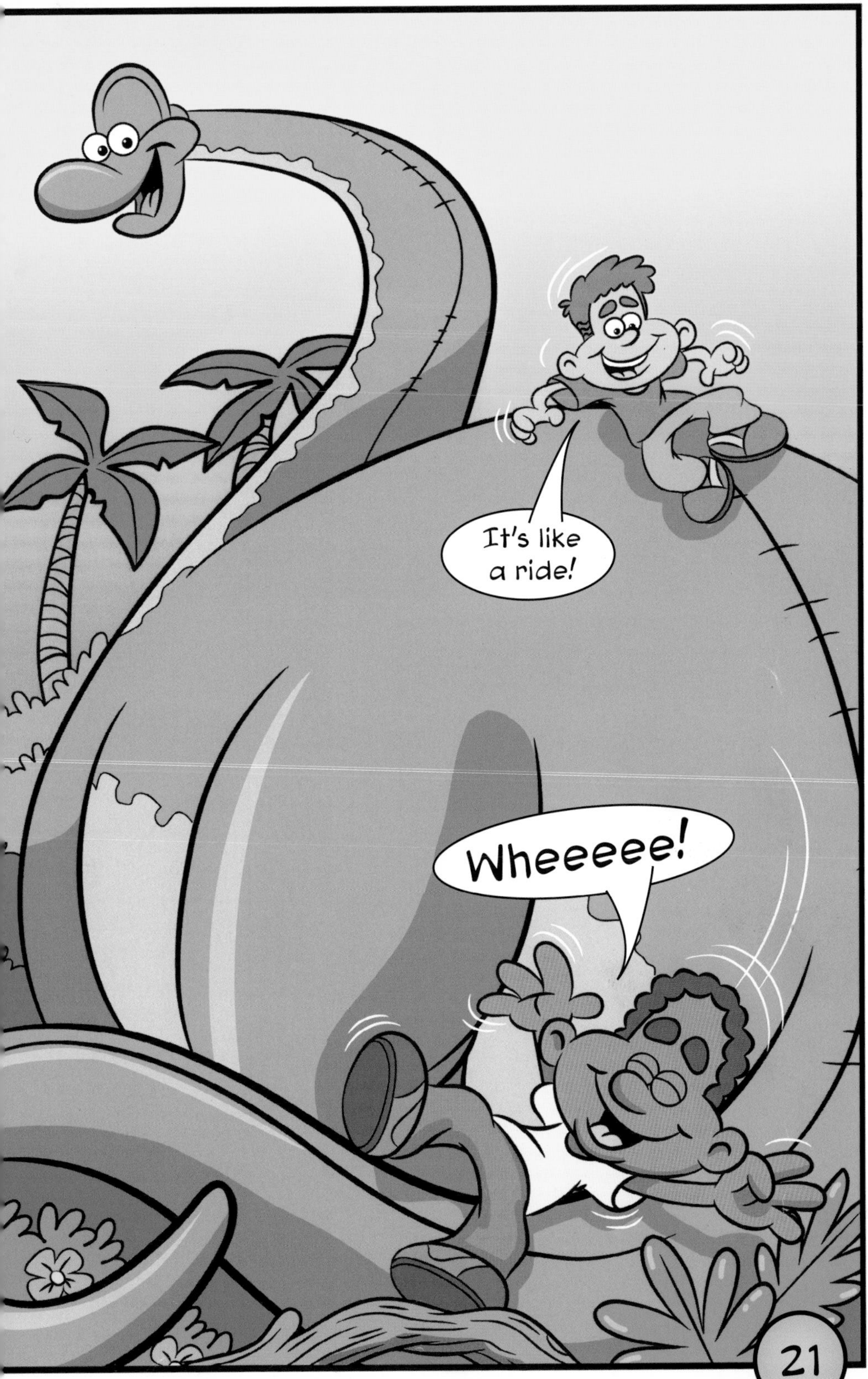
It's like a ride!
Wheeeee!

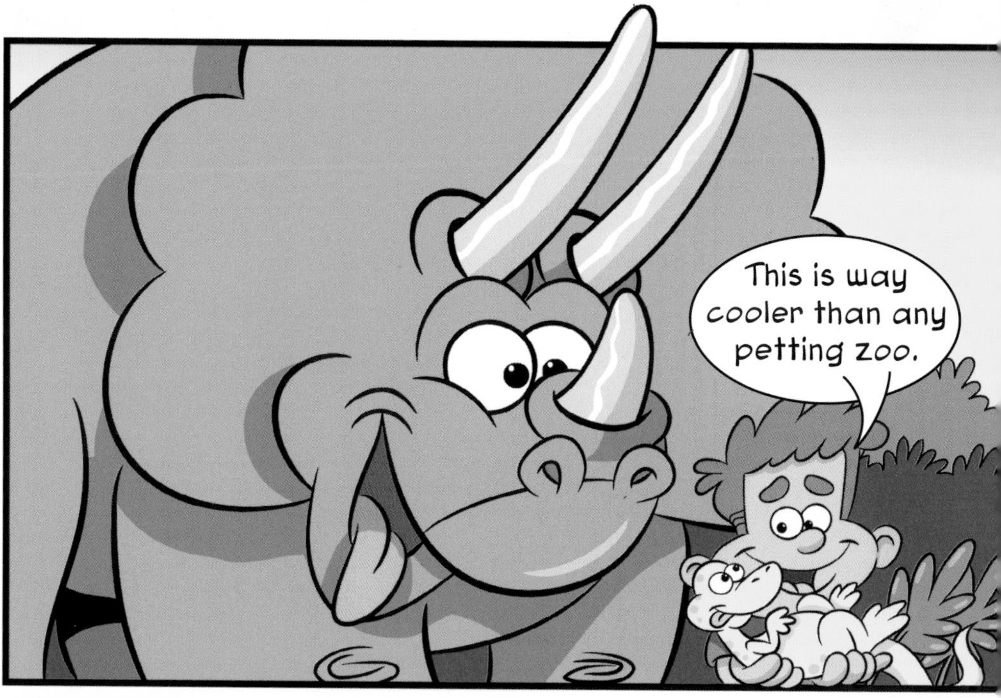
This is way cooler than any petting zoo.

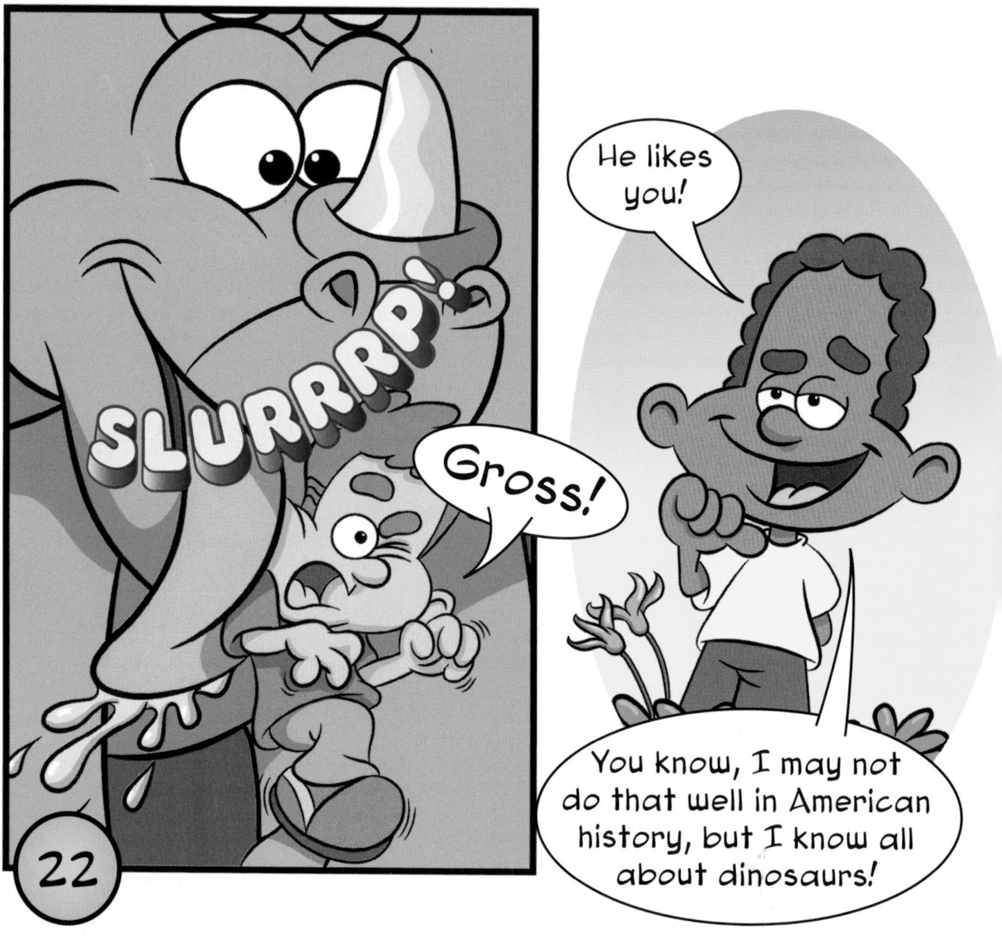
SLURRRP!
Gross!
He likes you!
You know, I may not do that well in American history, but I know all about dinosaurs!

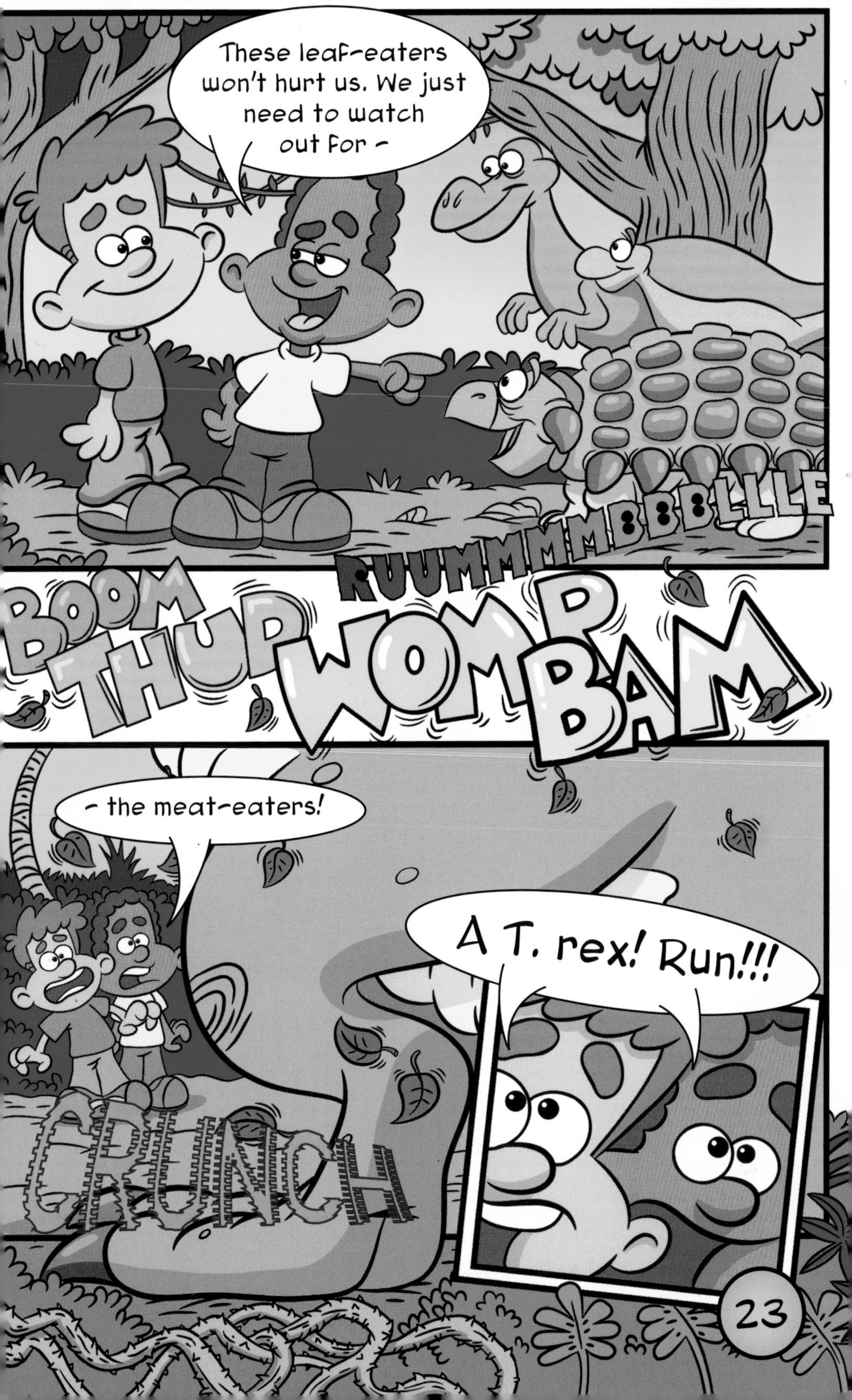
These leaf-eaters won't hurt us. We just need to watch out for -
RUUMMMMMBBBLLLE
BOOM
THUD
WOMP
BAM
- the meat-eaters!
A T. rex! Run!!!
CRUNCH

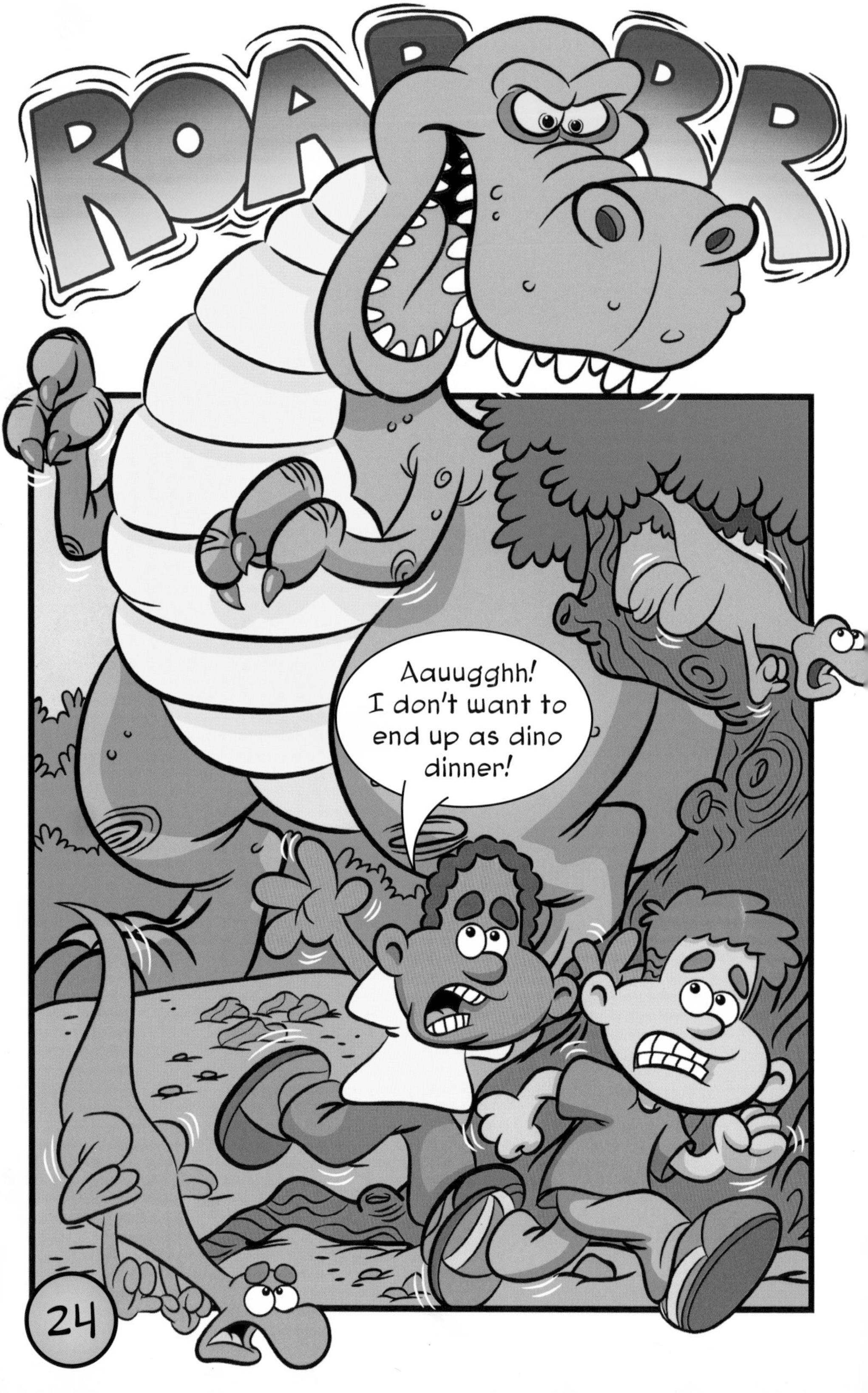
ROARRR
Aauugghh! I don't want to end up as dino dinner!

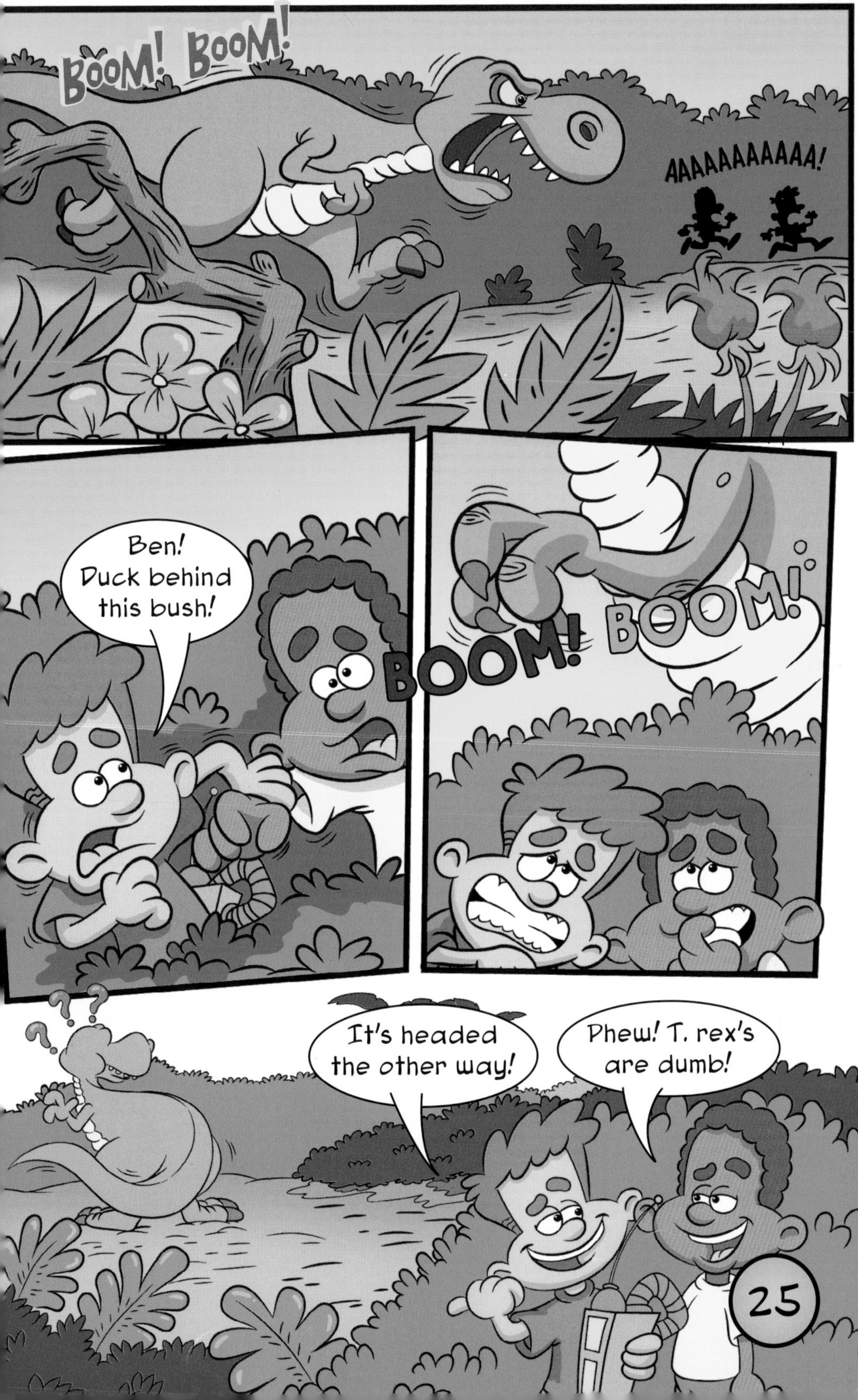
BOOM! BOOM!
AAAAAAAAAAA!
Ben! Duck behind this bush!
BOOM! BOOM!
It's headed the other way!
Phew! T. rex's are dumb!

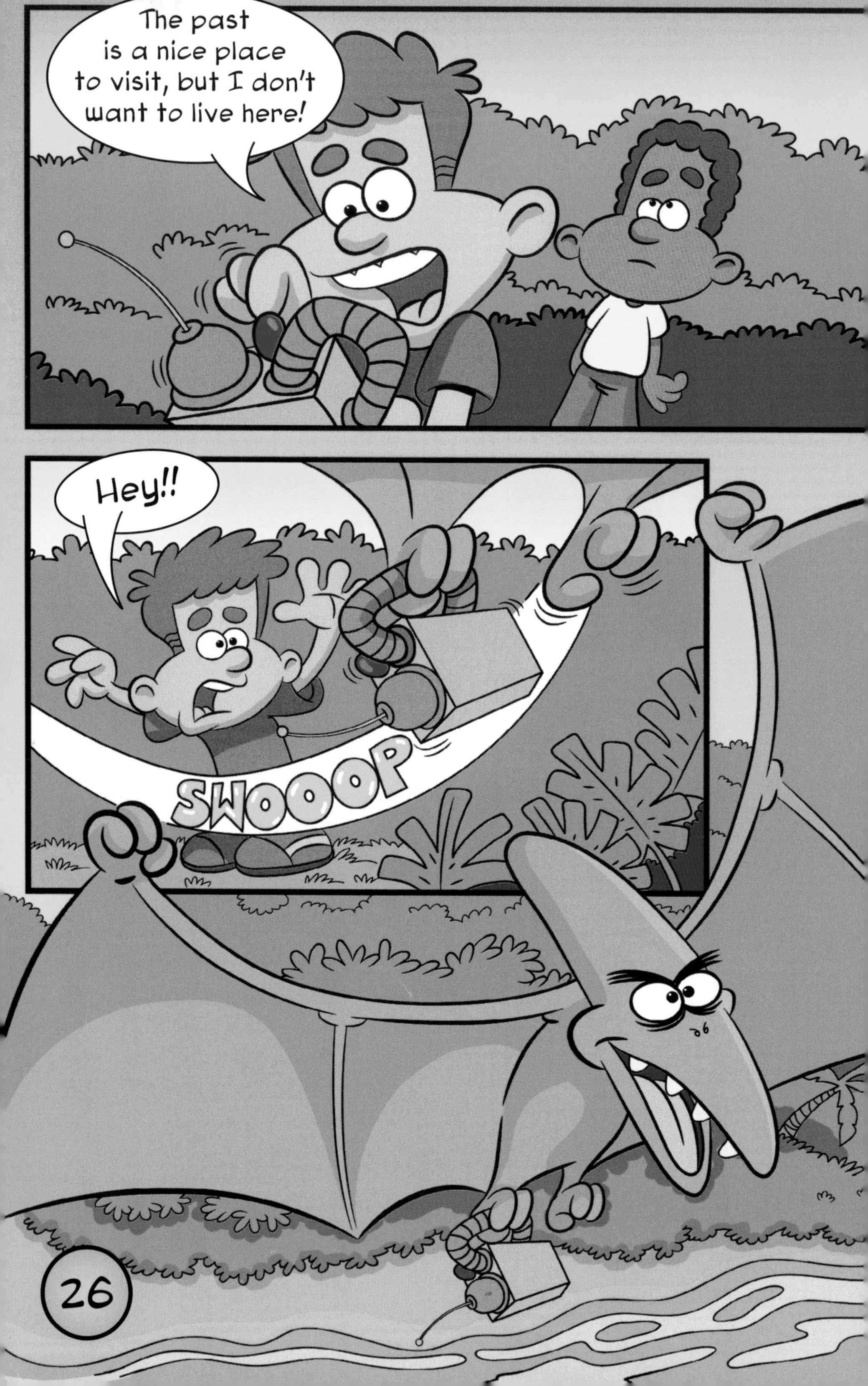
The past is a nice place to visit, but I don't want to live here!
Hey!!
SWOOOP

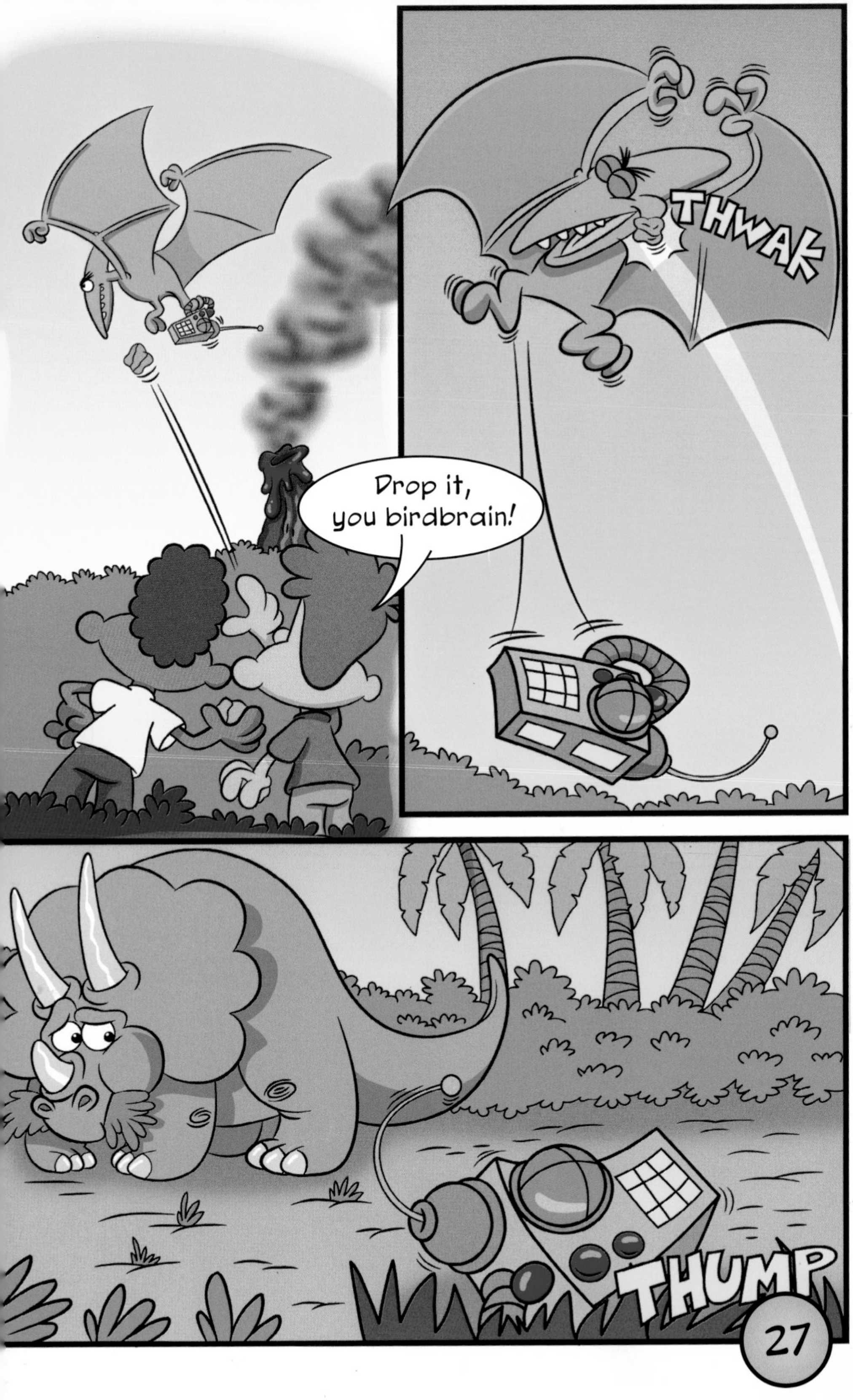
Drop it,
you birdbrain!
THWAK
THUMP

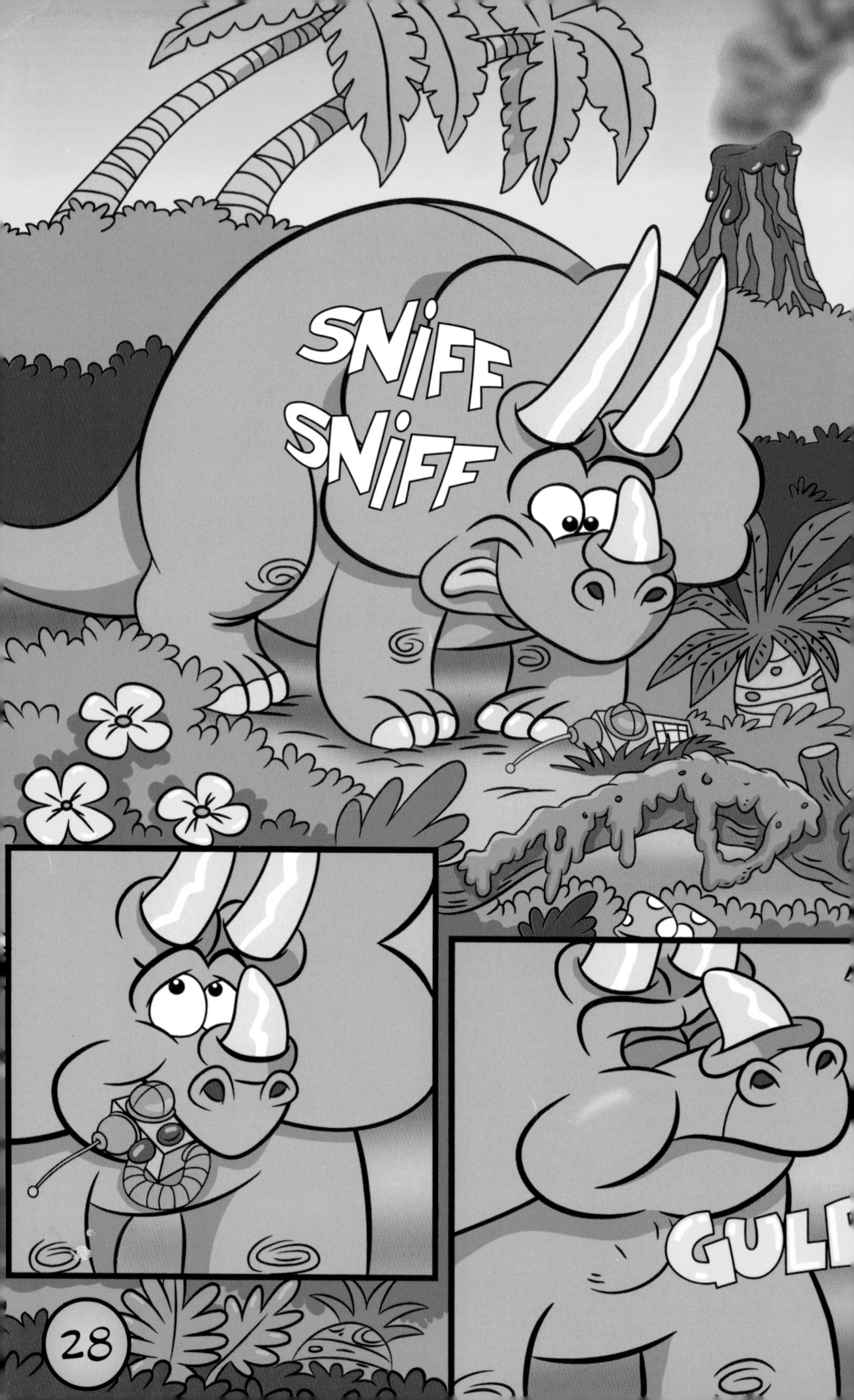
SNIFF
SNIFF
GUL

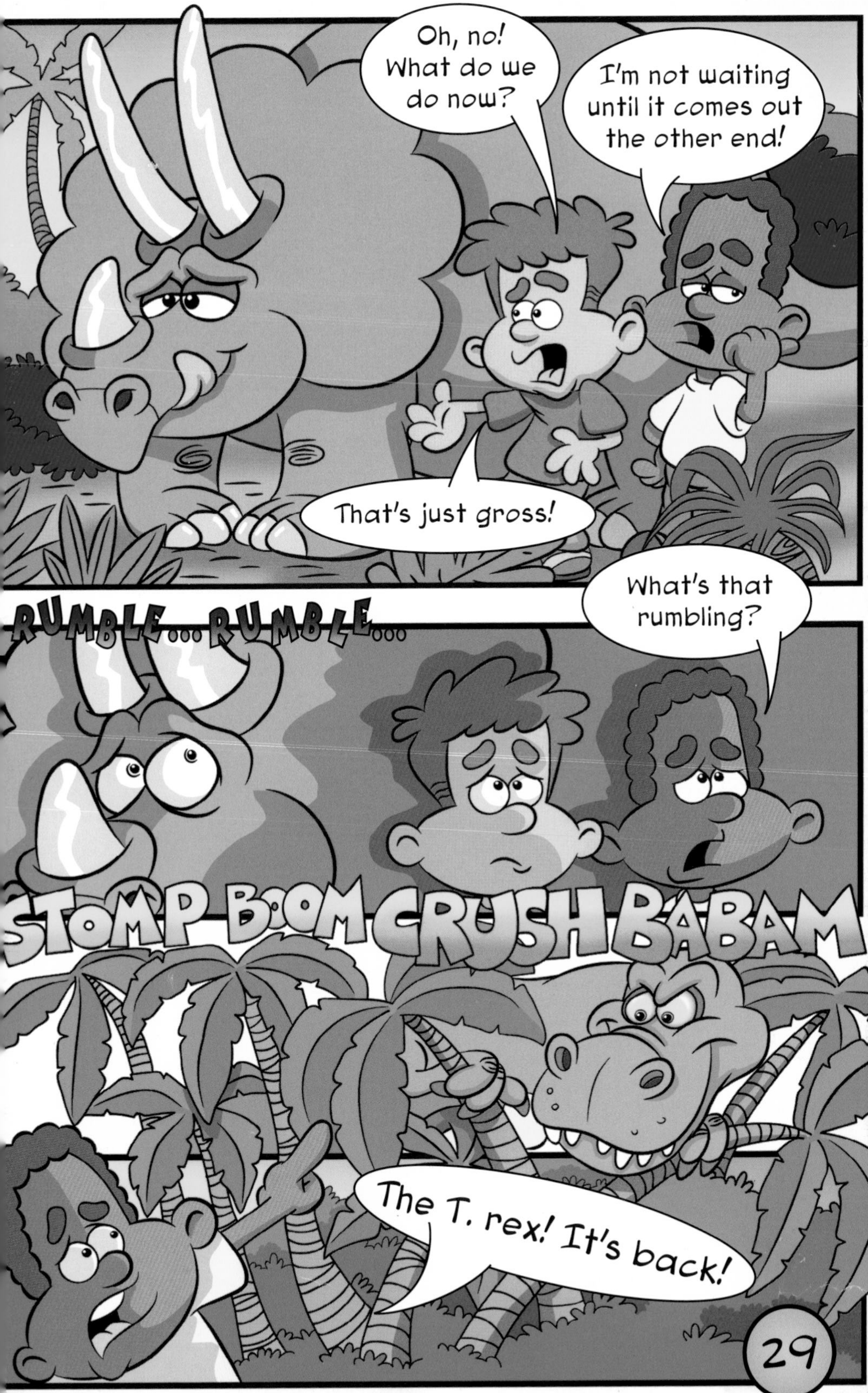
Oh, no! What do we do now?
I'm not waiting until it comes out the other end!
That's just gross!
RUMBLE... RUMBLE...
What's that rumbling?
STOMP BOOM CRUSH BABAM
The T. rex! It's back!

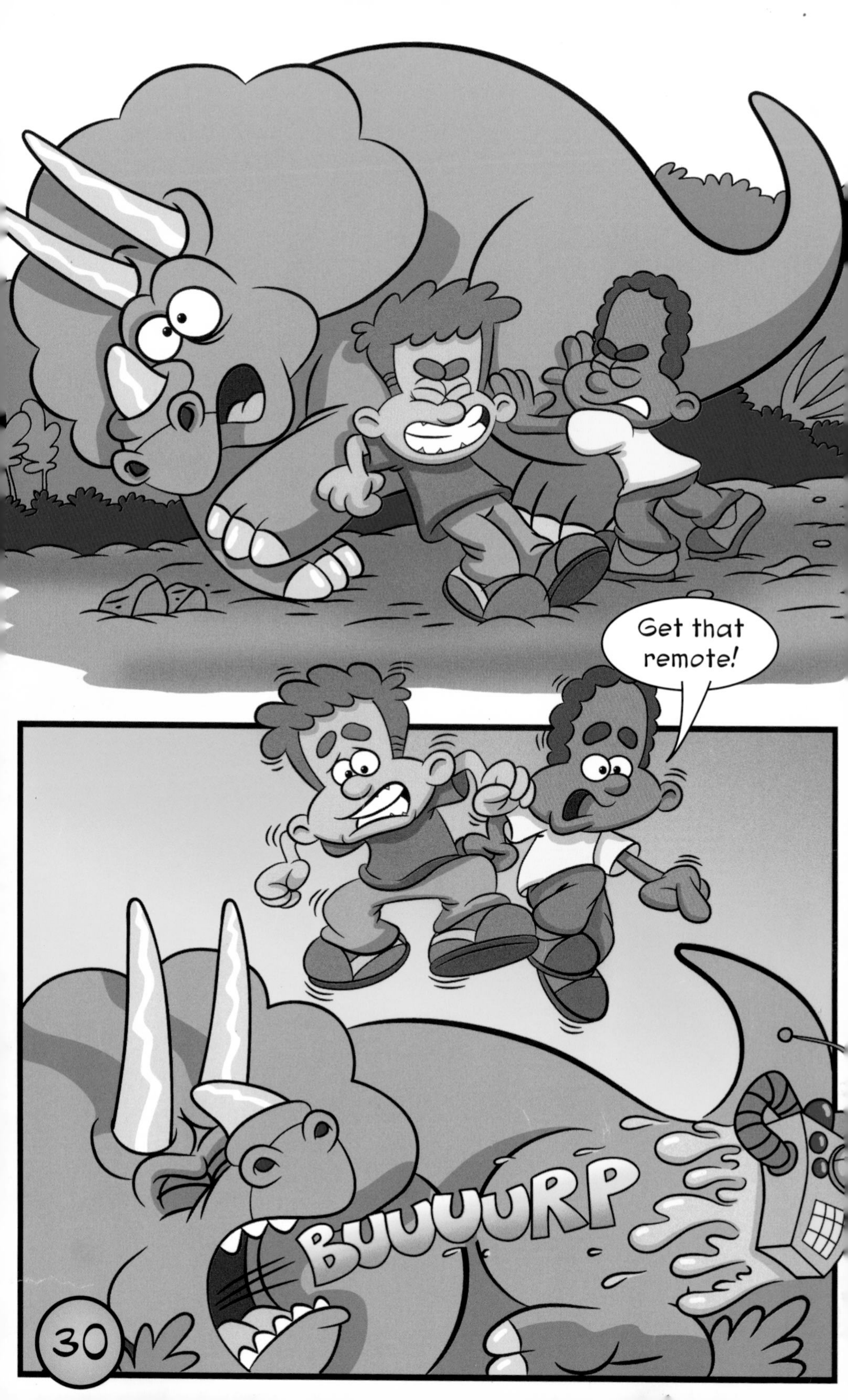
Get that remote!
BUUUURP

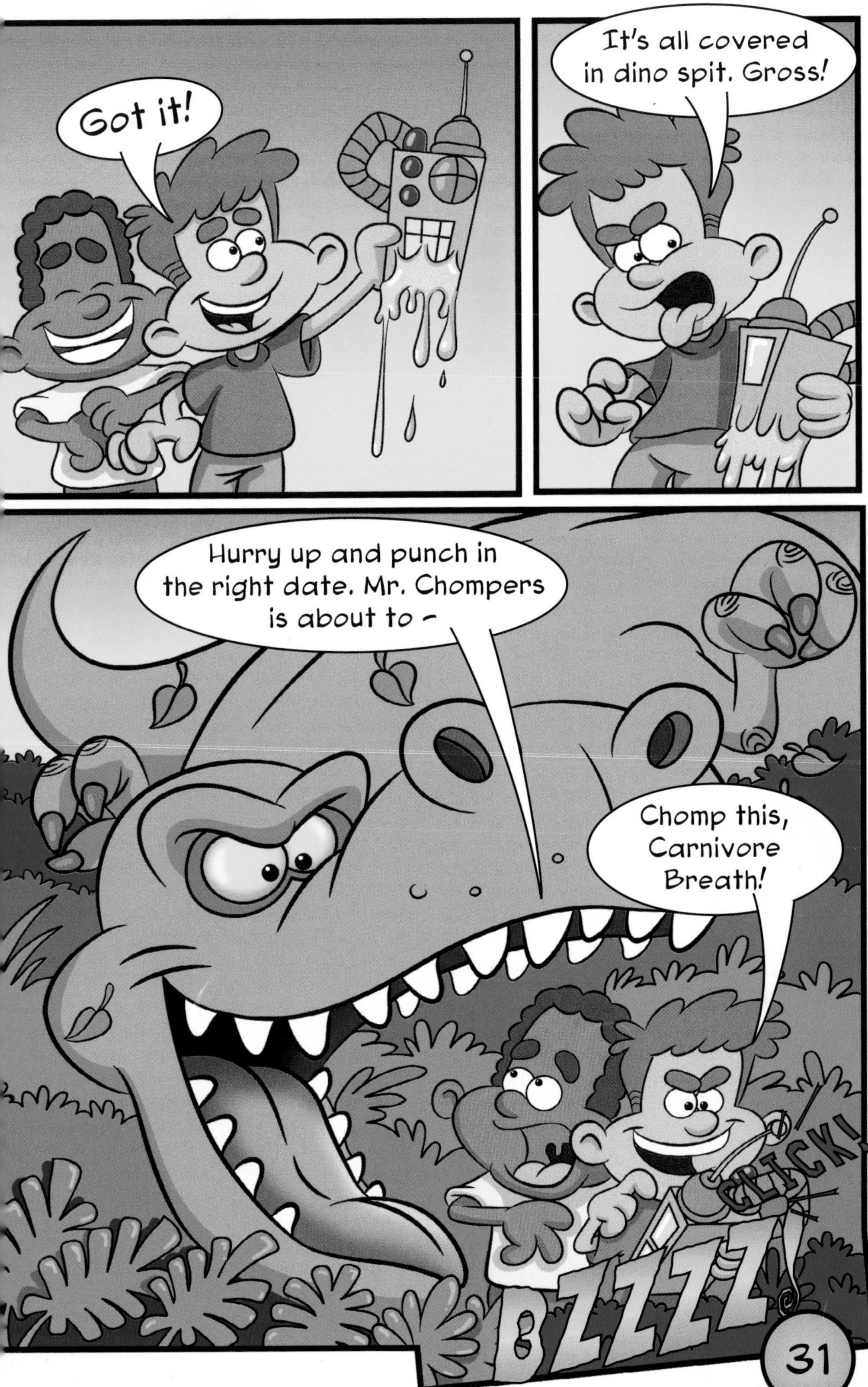
Got it!
It's all covered in dino spit. Gross!
Hurry up and punch in the right date. Mr. Chompers is about to -
Chomp this, Carnivore Breath!
CLICK!
BZZZZ

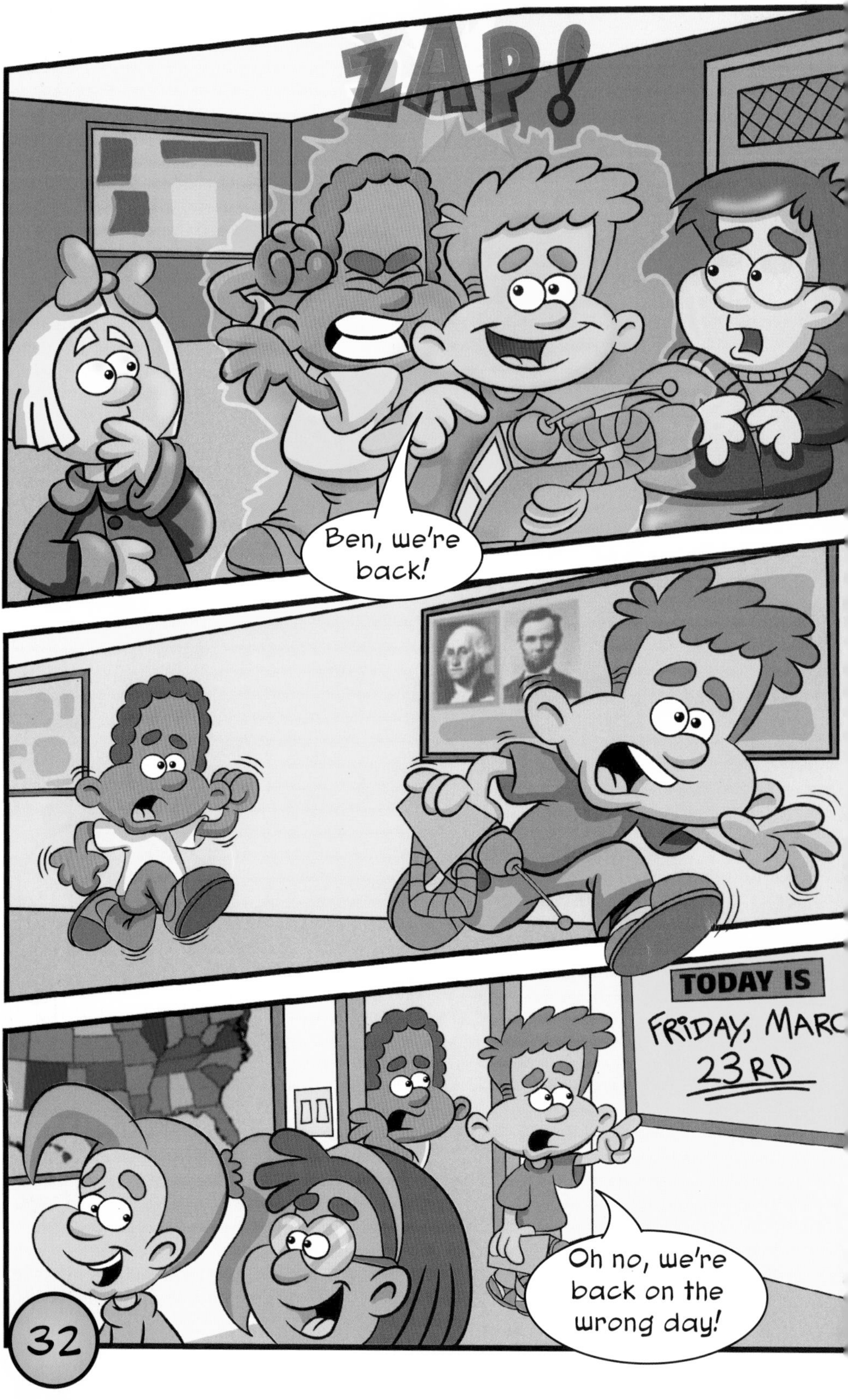
ZAP!
Ben, we're back!
TODAY IS
FRIDAY, MARC
23RD
Oh no, we're back on the wrong day!

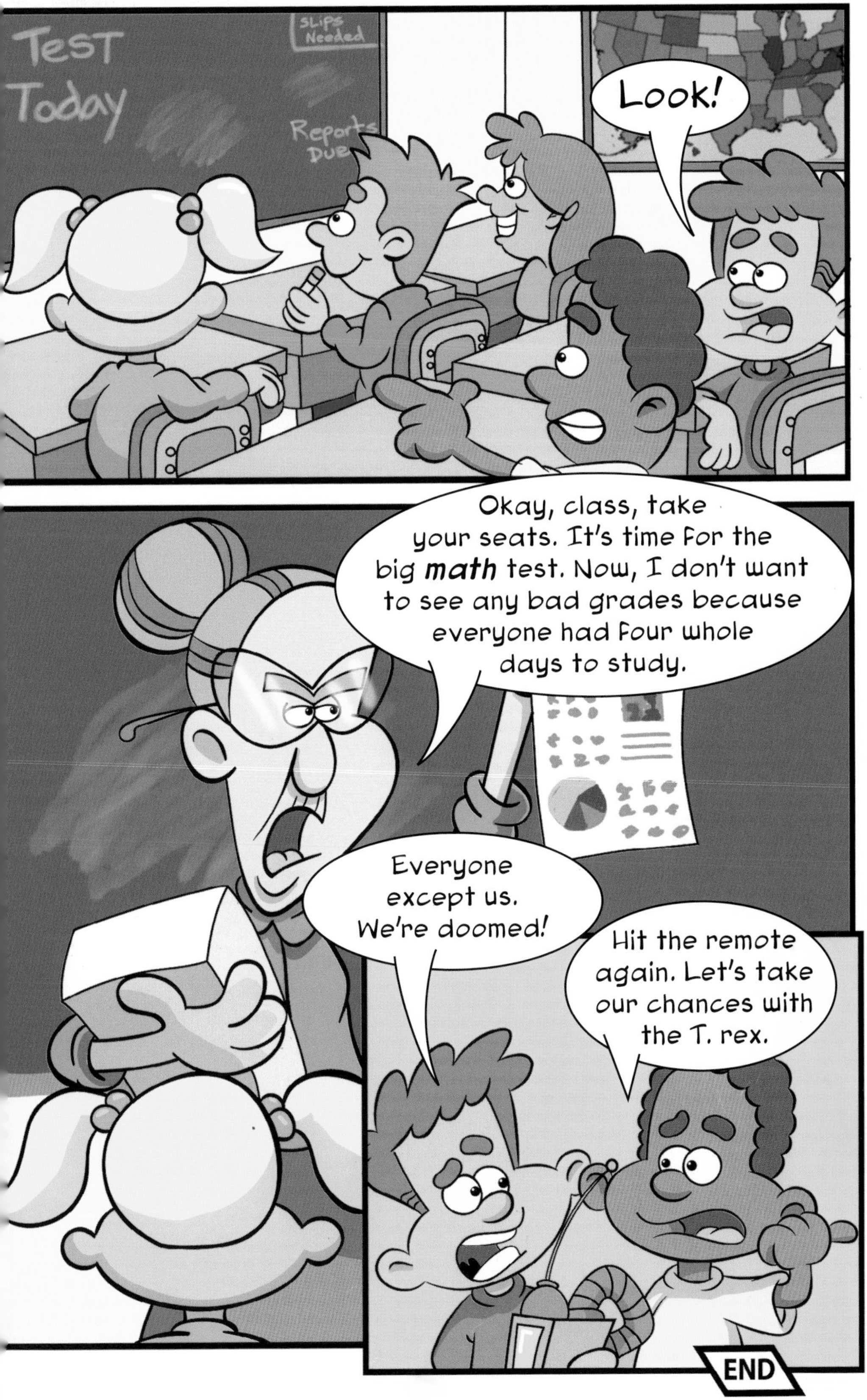
TEST Today
SLIPS Needed
Reports Due
Look!
Okay, class, take your seats. It's time for the big *math* test. Now, I don't want to see any bad grades because everyone had four whole days to study.
Everyone except us. We're doomed!
Hit the remote again. Let's take our chances with the T. rex.
END

ABOUT THE AUTHOR

Scott Nickel has written children's books, short fiction for *Boys' Life Magazine*, humorous greeting cards, and lots of really funny knock-knock jokes. Scott is also the author of many Garfield books.

Currently, Scott lives in Indiana with his wife, two sons, four cats, a parakeet, and several sea monkeys.

ABOUT THE ILLUSTRATOR

Steve Harpster has loved drawing funny cartoons, mean monsters, and goofy gadgets since he was able to pick up a pencil. In first grade, he was able to avoid his writing assignments by working on the pictures for stories instead.

Steve landed a job drawing funny pictures for books, and that's really what he's best at. Steve lives in Columbus, Ohio, with his wonderful wife, Karen, and their sheepdog, Doodle.

GLOSSARY

brachiosaur (BRAK-ee-uh-sor) a long-necked, plant-eating dinosaur that lived more than 150 million years ago

carnivore (KAR-nuh-vor) a meat-eater, like a *T. rex* or your dog

dino droppings (DYE-noh DROP-ingz) prehistoric poop, also known to scientists as coprolites (KOP-ruh-lites)

eek (EEK) the proper sound to make when you are frightened by the grade on your history test; "ack" will also work.

geek (GEEK) anyone who knows more about computers and science than you do

Ultra Galactic (UHL-truh guh-LAK-tik) the master, or highest, level on the Space Slime Commandos video game

zillionth (ZIL-yuhnth) a lot! More than a jillion, but not as such as a gazillion.

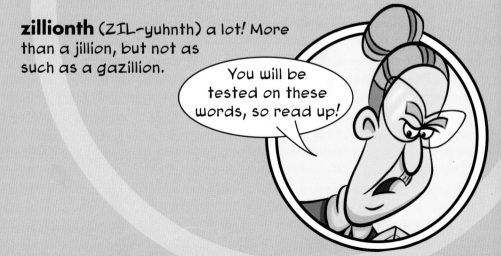

You will be tested on these words, so read up!

DINO BLASTS

WEIRD FACTS ABOUT DINOSAURS

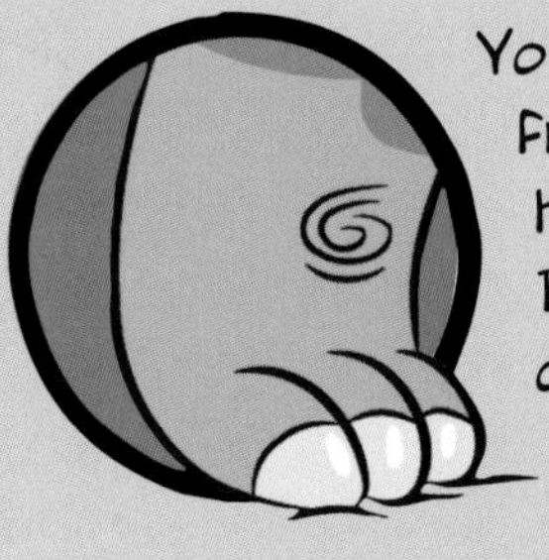

You can tell a plant-eating dinosaur from a meat-eater by noting how many legs they walked on. Plant-eaters usually stomped around on all four legs. Swift and deadly meat-eaters hunted on two legs.

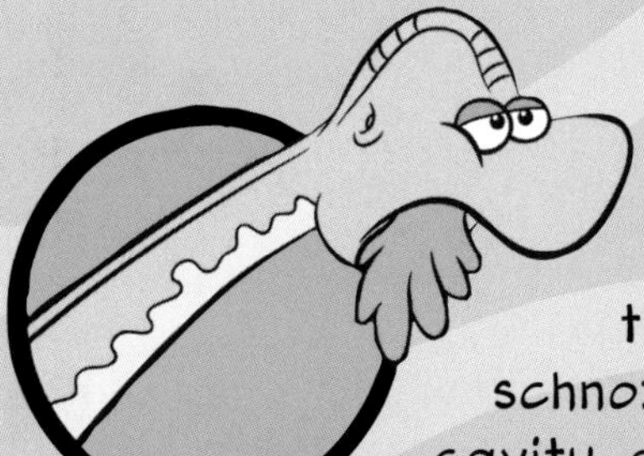

Brachiosaurus had nostrils on the top of its head. Some scientists think the placement of its schnozz, and its large nasal cavity, gave this plant-eater a strong sense of smell.

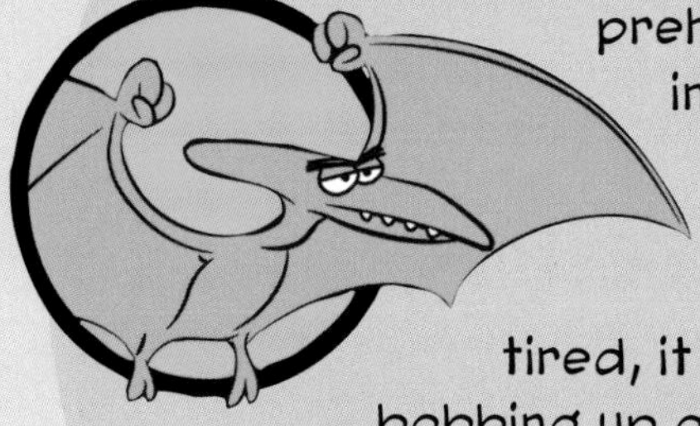

Pteranodon flew over the vast prehistoric oceans, diving into the water to snatch fish. Some scientists think that when this flying creature was tired, it sat on the waves, bobbing up and down like a cork or a duck. A big, ***big*** duck.

Tyrannosaurus rex had a mouthful of deadly teeth, which were shaped like bananas. But what's with those puny arms? Dino experts think the tiny paws meant that *T. rex* didn't fight for its food but ate creatures that were already dead. Yuck!

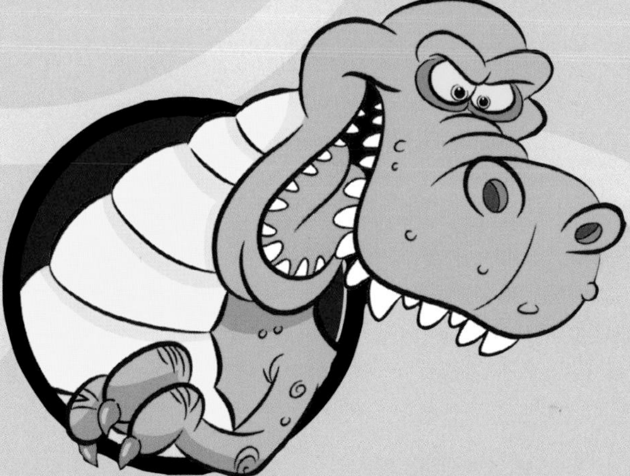

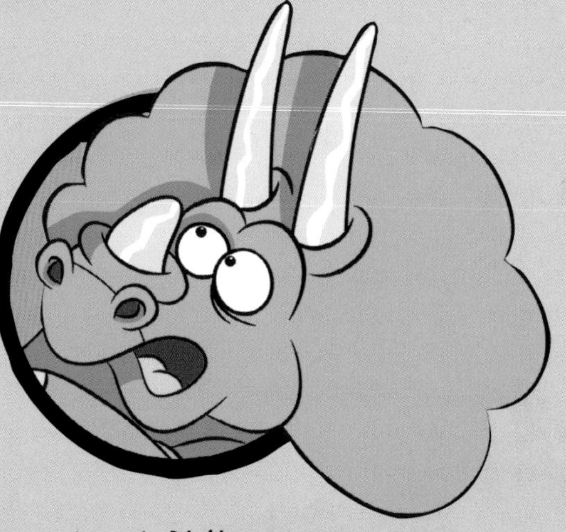

At least one *T. rex* has left its poop behind. Scientists examined the fossilized doo-doo and found bone fragments from a *Triceratops*. There's no word on whether this three-horned dino was alive or dead at the time of the meal.

DISCUSSION QUESTIONS

1.) If time machines really existed, would you use one to go back in time to retake a test? Do you think that would be fair?

2.) In books and movies, whenever humans and dinosaurs get together, the dinos attack the puny humans. Do you think this would really happen?

3.) If dinosaurs were available at the local pet store, which one would you want to take home, and why? How do you think your parents or friends would react to your new pet?

WRITING PROMPTS

1.) Everyone makes mistakes. If you could go back in time to visit one of your past mistakes, which mistake would you choose? Write about how you would fix it.

2.) David's geeky brother, Darrin, celebrated the invention of his time pod by making a giant egg-salad sandwich. If you were famous for creating an invention, write about what it would be. How would you celebrate?

3.) At a nearby mall, a time pod will be set up for willing customers. You can travel back to prehistoric time and see dinosaurs up close and personal. You can take three items along on your trip, but only three. Write about which ones you would take and why.

INTERNET

Do you want to know more about subjects related to this book? Or are you interested in learning about other topics? Then check out FactHound, a fun, easy way to find Internet sites.

Our investigative staff has already sniffed out great sites for you!

Here's how to use FactHound:

1.) Visit www.facthound.com

2.) Select your grade level.

3.) To learn more about subjects related to this book, type in the book's ISBN number: **1598890336**. If you're looking for information on another subject, simply type in a keyword.

4.) Click the *Fetch It* button.

FactHound will fetch the best Internet sites for you.